PRIME

NATE KENYON

PRIME

Copyright © 2009 by Nate Kenyon
Cover art "Cloning" © by Katja Faith
Interior art © by Mike Dominic
Cover design by Justin Stewart

Apex Publications, LLC
PO Box 24323
Lexington, KY 40524

www.apexbookcompany.com
www.natekenyon.com
katjafaith.deviantart.com

First Edition, July 2009

ISBN TPB: **978-0-9821596-2-0**

Printed in the United States of America

www.apexbookcompany.com

PRIME

NATE KENYON

An Apex Publications Book
Lexington, KY

To Emily, Harrison, and Abbey:
May your sandcastles never fall down.

Acknowledgments

I'd like to thank Jason Sizemore at Apex for his enthusiasm for my work and Deb Taber for her excellent editing skills.

I'd also like to thank my agent, Brendan Deneen at FinePrint Literary Management, for helping find this novella a home and for his constant support. He's one of the good guys, and I'm glad to have him in my corner.

"At this inflection point the world as we know it will change; real will mesh with virtual and life will bleed seamlessly into art until there are no longer any visible seams. Humankind will, at its Second Stage apex, become one with the machine, and will never look back."

—**Michael Gutenberg,** *Transformations: Book One*

BEFORE

Outside the shell, the machines were alive, swarming his flesh. They entered through his mouth and tumbled down his throat like a thousand tiny sand fleas, leaping and turning and wriggling, pumping oxygen into his lungs and cells, keeping his blood fresh and red. The nanomachines took to their duty like good little soldiers while the waveform manipulators washed his cortex, reading whatever blips remained and recording past histories.

His chest rose and fell, muscles twitched, an eyelid fluttered, and imagination took flight within the dreams of men.

Inside, all was still and dark and empty.

—§—

"He's gone, then?"

"Not quite. We can detect a bit of activity, but it's not clear what's left."

"Could see it coming. He lost focus."

"Love will do that to you."

The figure standing before the glass sighed. "What was recovered, then?"

"Memories. Fragments. I'll show you."

The glass flickered as a holodeck unit hissed to life. The projected image showed a darkened room and a man strapped to a chair, arms cuffed behind his back. His head was down, and although his chest moved, he gave no indication of consciousness.

A second man entered the projected room, and then a third. They approached the man in the chair, speaking in a Cantonese dialect, and then one of them kicked the legs of the chair away so that the prisoner fell backward to the floor.

"*Siu sam!*" the other said. *Be careful.*

The other one laughed. "*Nei bin do tung?*" he said to the man in the chair. "*Nei sui yiu hui chi soh ma?*"

The man on the floor moaned. "Don't," he said. His voice was barely audible. "Please."

"English?" The one who had kicked him stepped closer. "You no tell us who hire you, you hurt more. I take finger." He took out a laser blade. "I cut one, two. Maybe more. Maybe here next." He gestured to his own crotch. "You like?"

"I..." The prisoner tried to move away, pushing his legs weakly against the floor, but the chair kept him

2

still. "I'll tell you. Just please..."

"Yes?" The man with the blade leaned in. "You talk now. Name?"

Abruptly, the man on the floor thrust up from his hips and lashed out with a vicious kick, his foot snapping the other man's head back and driving the cartilage of his nose deep into his brain. He flexed his arms and the chair frame cracked, and as his adversary fell dead he was already free of the chair and looping his cuffed arms underneath and around his legs to his front.

The second man who had entered the room turned to run. The cuffed man was on him in seconds, flicking his hands over the fleeing man's neck and pulling the chain taut.

Silence fell, broken only by the choking sounds that slowly died away—and then a second body falling lifeless to the floor.

The cuffed man listened for a moment, then returned to the first body and picked up the laser blade. A quick twist of the blade in his hands and the cuffs fell free.

He stood among the dead and smiled.

—§—

"Stop it there, please," said the man standing at the glass. The holodeck image froze. "Impressive."

"He was hired to take down a virus that had disabled

half the East Coast network. These men were members of the group that unleashed it. He went in afterward and killed the bug in record time, then found the rest of the group and terminated them. He was gone before they'd even started to clean up the mess."

"Hmmm. How do we know he's not playing possum now?"

"His waveforms are practically flatlined."

"We didn't see this sort of effort before."

"He's been compromised. Lost focus, as you said. I have other examples of his skill—"

"No, that's enough. You think we still need him. Can he be revived?"

"I don't know."

The man at the glass studied the supine figure on the table. "All right. We have what we want. If this is an insurance policy, have at it, whatever you need to do. Just don't let the whole thing come back to bite us."

The man stepped away and left the room. After a few moments the second man who had spoken approached the barrier. He stared at the prisoner on the table. "Thank you," he whispered.

As he watched the nanomachines do their work, his finger absently traced the circle and arrow pattern etched into the glass.

Chapter 1
AFTER

Six years later

The two women were historians and as they entered the nesting cubicle, they were deep in a heated discussion about meat as art. "Fischer's oils create a visceral response," one said. "Raw flesh becomes an object of worship, whereas with Sterbak it's often more about human flesh and our response as it is presented under circumstances that are jarring to the viewer. It's the difference between consumption for sustenance versus sexual pleasure. You see?"

"I wouldn't call her *House of Pain* sexual."

"Ah, but that's exactly it." The two women settled back in soft, contoured zero-gravity chairs, their weight perfectly balanced within the contact suits they wore like second skins. The cubicle was bare, the smooth cream walls meant to swallow noise and reflect sensation. It was rented by the hour. "Sex and death. Ever read *The Tears of Eros?* They're inextricably linked."

"Bataille was a surrealist."

"Only when it was convenient." The second woman, taller and nicely plump, rubbed her ample breasts. "These suits always make me feel like I'm wearing nothing at all. Are you ready, Dobs?"

Deborah nodded and handed her the headgear. "I want a tall one this time, a royal perhaps, with chest hair."

The plump woman, whose name was Stephie, slipped the gear over her head and settled it into place. No corneal implants for either of them, at least not yet, although Deborah finally could have afforded something like that after all these years.

She looked at Stephie. So enthusiastic, like a child with a new toy. A net virgin until university, born to card-carrying members of the virtual resistance who were obsessed with organic cloned fruits, historical recreations of eighteenth century France, and leg hair, the experience was still relatively new to her. Deborah assumed that the history degree in twenty-first century art had been her rebellion. She seemed to be making up for lost time.

Stephie's voice came muffled from within; they hadn't established a com-link yet. "Sustenance versus sexual pleasure, indeed. I'm thinking Nordic, with a fighter's build—"

"That's what you always choose!"

"And a brooding, artistic type. Eric Bloodaxe and Poe. Wouldn't it be fun to have an intellectual discussion with one while the other bends you over a chair?"

Deborah giggled. "You're so *dirty*, Stephie."

"We're on vacation. I feel it's appropriate."

"I suppose I need to invest in my own equipment."

"Then you'd use it all the time," Stephie said. "I'm not ready to give up on the physical, regardless of what our lovely government is preaching, but the temptation would be too much if it were right in front of me. As Gutenberg has made abundantly clear, once the illusion of reality is seamless, humanity will have difficulty finding reason to return. You've experienced his *Transformations*, haven't you?"

Deborah nodded. Of course she had; everyone had at least once, even the non-believers. She had experienced it originally as a historian concerned with understanding the modern belief structures of humanity. She was not one to attach herself to religious movements; she considered herself a practical person. But she had to admit that the idea of Transforming was, regardless of her natural aversion to technology, quite appealing.

"Are there really natural sensitives?"

"Of course there are. I saw a documentary on one just the other day. I asked the AI what it was like, and he said it was just like experiencing a serotonin dip."

"He was pulling your leg."

7

"I asked for an immersive, and he showed it to me. Seamless: blinking in, blinking out, as natural as breathing."

The lights in the room began to dim. Deborah sighed and adjusted her gear as the link popped. Stephie's voice was inside her head. "See you on the other side, Dobs."

The room went black. Deborah felt the familiar sensation of panic as her senses reacted to the lack of stimuli. The feeling of floating through endless space made her want to jerk out her arms and legs for balance like a sleeping child falling from bed. Sterback would have enjoyed an experience like this, Deborah thought, sexual expression that was real and yet not real. Would she have studied the reactions of users and considered them authentic? The ability to control an encounter compromised the experiment, perhaps. No matter how far you took it, there was always the safety net.

Sex and death. Two of humankind's most powerful experiences. It was no wonder so many got the two confused.

—§—

Sometime later, Deborah said goodbye to her version of King Henry the Eighth, who had become tiresome. She had thought it would be good fun and a bit of a dangerous thrill to be intimate with such a legendary rogue, one whom she had spent so many years study-ing. But after their initial conversations about the Bo-leyn sisters and the torture and execution of John Fisher, she found him terminally boring. The program could draw from recorded history, but it was unable to make him react with truly unexpected responses the way a real human would. He could not tell her with any conviction how the colors on his feasting room walls made him feel, nor describe the smell of torchlight at an execution. Besides, she was feeling sore.

Stephie, on the other hand, seemed to have an end-less appetite for these sorts of encounters, as if her parents' resistance fighting had given her an addict's temperament. Deborah switched off the gear and let the blackness envelop her for a moment, enjoying the floating, disconnected feeling as much as anything that had come before it. She talked a good game for Stephie's sake, but, truth be told, she would rather spend her days buried among the actual pages of old books than inside the net. She'd grown up among the orphanages of Bangalore, where instead of ubiquitous net access they had a room full of books nobody had any use for anymore, old-fashioned novels and illus-trated art history encyclopedias with vivid full color prints. Her early schooling had been taken with Indian slave traders, between hours of begging for assistance for her father, crippled from the war—a father who did not actually exist.

Perhaps that was why she and Stephie got along so

well, she thought. They had hit it off instantly when they'd met in a class on the impact of Tata's Nano on the population explosion and industrialization of the Third World. Perhaps by then they had been the last two net virgins on earth.

Even through the lack of any external stimuli, floating weightless in the void, Deborah imagined she could feel the city of New London rising up around her, steaming streets full of the heat and humidity of nearly constant rain since the collapse of Old Greenland, the smell of twenty million humans, stray dogs, and garbage filling her nostrils. This was her third trip to New London, and she found it terrifying. Giant OLED video screens and holographic projectors streamed customized infomercials and dark marketing broadcasts twenty-four hours a day. The latest wave technology beamed some of them straight into the brain like tiny focused lasers of capitalism. They seemed to know Deborah's every whim and wish before she knew herself, and the alternate reality games made her thirst to buy things. Stephie said they were altering her alphas without her consent, although that was supposedly illegal. She didn't like the feeling. It was more than a little unsettling for a woman who had lived unplugged for a good portion of her early life.

But Stephie embraced all new experiences with her typical gusto, her appetites huge, her enthusiasm limitless. Deborah was more than a little in love with her. Not in a sexual way, of course. And anyway, she would never say such a thing out loud.

When King Henry had sufficiently faded from memory and she had removed her gear, the first thing she noticed was the heat in the room. It seemed to have risen twenty degrees.

She turned to Stephie, but it was too dark to see much other than the vague outline of her body. She seemed to be jerking back and forth.

"Steph?" Deborah whispered, wondering if she were out of the sim. But no, she could just see the suggestion of headgear over her companion's face. Stephie was still inside.

There was a smell in the air. *Burnt hair?* Not quite. Deborah pinched her nostrils shut. It was growing stronger by the minute. Something was wrong.

"Lights," she said, but nothing happened. She tried to get up, but the zero-gravity chair made it nearly impossible. The controls weren't working at all, and knowing she was inside a seven foot square cubicle didn't help.

A sudden tingle in the fingers of her right hand made her realize she was still holding onto the headgear. The tingle came again, much stronger this time, and she threw the gear against the wall like she'd been scalded. Her friend thrashed more violently. "Stephie!" she shouted, rolling against the contoured surfaces of the chair—*damn these armrests*—until she rolled over the edge and onto the floor with a thump.

Sex and death, Deborah thought, for reasons she

only vaguely understood. She got to her feet with the smell of burning flesh in her nostrils and realized that she could see now because Stephie's hair was on fire.

Deborah screamed, but the room's acoustics deadened the sound. Drawn forward by a mixture of fascination and dread—driven by an animalistic urge to know, to see—she leaned over her friend's body. It had arched upward so far it was as if Stephie's spine had cracked. Her lips had peeled back from her teeth in a rictus of pleasure or pain, and her skin was blistering and turning black amid the flickering flames.

Chapter 2

The building's sheath was as slick-shiny as a salamander's skin. It thrust up from the sea in a wash of organic colors, flashing with the occasional blue and blood lights of passing Privates and the brilliant flood beams of larger Carriers, and looked like the tail of a monstrous scorpion sticking up out of the ground, quivering and many-jointed and poised to sting.

New London Tower: the centerpiece, the power source, and the heart of the vast city.

William Bellow stood one hundred feet away and breathed the salt air. He'd come many miles today, and he was tired and hungry and covered with a thin sheen of sweat. He held an old leather valise in his right hand, the kind with straps and metal buckles. It matched his well-worn façade just fine. He had bought it at an antiques shop in Singapore; the old lady who sold it to him had spoken some sort of dialect that he had barely understood.

PRIME

"Sic-sicca lau lee." Your face is dangerous. He'd understood that much. Perhaps she'd seen him on the news. He had paid her in New London credits and tried not to notice as she shied away from his touch.

"It ain't going to bite, old man," said a passing teen in a textured work suit. The kid grinned. "Not from here, anyway." Pressure points stood out like rubber nipples all over his scrawny body. His scalp was palmed by the tattooed holographic image of a hand, the pads of black fingertips resting upon his brows as if holding them up in an expression of permanent surprise.

The boy slipped away on hoverblades. Bellow watched the window facets carefully, as if searching for any response. The skyscraper remained impassive. It was only a shell. What he had come for was inside.

"You must be Will," the impeccably dressed building manager said. He introduced himself as Harry Crowther. He was wearing a navy smart suit complete with white handkerchief and gold cuffs, and he looked suitably middle-aged and recently combed and styled, although the grooming looked hastily done. Maybe he'd been interrupted from a nap.

"I was expecting someone..." He couldn't seem to come up with an appropriate qualifier. "You know how it is these days. Surfing at five, programming worldwide

at fifteen. Burned out at twenty-one. Or retired." He smiled.

Something about his face looked familiar. Bellow volunteered nothing of his former life and what had landed him there; Crowther probably knew most of it anyway. Bellow knew what he looked like: a decade older than he was with wrinkles around the edges of his eyes and lips, hair gone slightly gray at the temples, a dinosaur in the age of limitless beauty and eternal life—at least for the wealthy. Perversely, the women liked him better for it.

"I was pleased to hear you were coming to visit us," the manager said. "I'd thought you would simply jack in from outside."

"I like to get a feel for a place. The people who take care of it. You can learn a lot from the amount of dust on a floor."

"I suppose that's true," Crowther said, as if he had a good idea of what Bellow meant. "We're only so good as our cleaning crew, isn't that right? Attention to detail, in this day and age, is a necessity, isn't it? We're all so *busy*, life is so *crowded*, the division of labor becomes all the more important. And one must take responsibility for his area of expertise. There is no time or consideration for a lack of effort."

They walked through the lobby and past the sentry bot. Bellow felt the brief warmth of a retina scan as the squat and spiderlike sentry paused, touched his corneal implants, and then moved on. He blinked into the web and probed gently against the gelatinous Tower firewalls, just enough to gather a list of names. He was already flagged in the security database, and while the news did not really surprise him, it was irritating. He never liked them to know he was coming.

He blinked out, into another hallway. They passed by several large workspaces with crowded holographic terminals and what seemed like hundreds of padded design cubicles full of kids in hotsuits and headgear. The boy from the street flashed him a brief smile and wink as he walked by, as if they shared some private joke.

"Ninety-seven floors," Crowther rattled on. "Medical implants, gene therapy, nanotech, quantum design—we do it all here. Then, of course, the owner-occupied suites on the upper, er, levels. And we are a fully functional programming and broadcasting center. Entertainment and shopping, mostly, but we also run a few business sites. Attendance at our seminars is up twenty percent—I'm sorry, am I boring you? I do go on. It's more than my business, it's my passion. Which is why I'm so concerned about the recent trouble."

"I'd like to see the main server."

"It's in the sub-basement. Access is restricted. I'll have to make a call. Excuse me a moment." He removed a slender holo-screen from his pocket and spoke a few words into it. A stream of dialogue followed from a floating female hologram.

"We're cleared to go," Crowther said.

PRIME

They took the express to the lower levels. As the doors slid silently open, the sentry bots were there in force, more insistent this time, scanning body crevices and taking DNA samples from a puff of skin cells. They waited while a bot analyzed Bellow's DNA results and scanned for organic explosives and designer drugs, then passed through steel doors and into a giant vibrating cylinder along a polymer-reinforced catwalk that circled the walls. The server hung suspended and humming beneath them like some monstrous sleeping child, capable of a hundred billion functions per millisecond, able to reveal worlds and then destroy them in the blink of an eye, her countless arms of magnetic layered quantum chips and alpha waves reaching out and linking virtual fingers with anyone who paid the subscribers' fee.

Ignoring the manager's surprised shout, Bellow leaned over the rail and placed both palms gently against the vibrating surface.

He slipped beneath the circular room and the smells of hot grease and electric current, or rather deep within it. There was a certain pitch that carried a voice and a presence only he could hear. The language was foreign but soothingly familiar, as if he were a fetus listening in the womb to his mother's muffled conversation. He became a part of the machinery, inserting himself into the hot coils and slippery chips, all the while probing ever deeper, ever closer to that something he sought.

There. Bellow imagined a tremor so slight it was not mechanical but magnetic. Then Crowther's slender, manicured hands were pulling him away from the machine, and he was once again on the catwalk with the manager's yapping, nervous face peering into his own as if searching for signs of mania.

"Are you *insane?* That's a two hundred foot drop!"

"Take your hands off me."

"I didn't mean any harm." The manager stepped back quickly and sputtered, red-faced, his calm façade cracked wide open. "You surprised me, that's all. I'd heard you were eccentric, had unusual methods, but this is a restricted area with sensitive equipment, you understand. Imagine introducing your child to me, and I slap my hands down on it without so much as a word. It's rather barbaric."

Christ, Bellow thought. *He's offended.* You had to be careful with these people; they operated within a very rigid social order, and they were fragile. But there was something funny about this man struggling to keep his emotions in check. As if a manager's blind-eyed professionalism would keep the entire vast expanse up and running.

On the way back to the upper levels, Bellow pretended to study his datapad, giving the building manager time to recover himself.

"You're aware that we've had some...incidents," Crowther said as they walked past the sentry clones. "Assuming our Board of Directors agrees, I'll brief you in full and open access to our files after you accept our binding security documents. These incidents are extremely sensitive, and we trust you won't speak of them to anyone. For now, you only need to know what the newsclips have reported to understand why you have been brought in here."

"A bug in the system. I felt it back there."

The manager looked at him blankly. "I'm sure that's impossible. The, er, bug is simply an electronic glitch."

"Your glitch has killed three people."

"The fact of the matter is that we service millions every day. A scant few of our users have received injuries from an unknown source. I'm not prepared to concede that it's even from our system."

Bellow shrugged. Three New London users had received roughly fifty thousand volts through the brain, according to his information, the last of them just yesterday. But who was he to argue?

They entered the elevator and the pneumatic doors whooshed shut. "There's the matter of my payment."

"I've been authorized to offer you up to two hundred thousand credits. Half up front, half upon completion of the job. You will be put up in our best suite, of course."

"I'd rather stay downtown. Helps me think."

"We'd prefer you keep a low profile. I'd have to authorize it—"

"I don't give a damn what you have to do," Bellow said. "This is what I want: three hundred thousand credits, one hundred thousand up front; money for traveling expenses; and freedom to operate without someone looking over my shoulder every five minutes."

"Is there something I've done to offend you?"

"I don't like building managers. The last one I knew tried to have me lobotomized."

The manager looked offended again and said he would have to make another call. *They'll do it*, Bellow thought, simply because they had no choice. Murder was not a game, and he was still the best, no matter how long it had been.

He was also the only one desperate or stupid enough to take the job.

Chapter 3

The New London board was a group of ten perfectly manipulated humans: every genetic flaw excised, every mole or sign of age erased. One of them had the pink, freshly scrubbed look of a recent micropore flush, as millions of nano-machines finished their programmed duties and returned in a dust-mote swarm to a shirt-pocketed vial.

They looked like cartoon characters, Bellow thought. He was seated in silence at a Bubinga wood conference table with Dunami massaging chairs, placed before a wall of polished glass with the tray ceiling at least twenty feet overhead. Personally, he'd take a slightly crooked nose and a little fat around the middle, and the hell with living forever. Too much re-sculpting and the edges started to blend together. Pretty soon you've lost sight of the original.

Someone expressed the possibility that the attacks

were the work of a member of the religious right. The Church of Transformations' explosive growth threatened the conservatives, and it made them much more aggressive as increasing numbers of people left them and joined Gutenberg's disciples. Such people might be inside New London—or might have hacked in.

Another board member suggested the underground resistance, the "antisprawl" movement. These people were, for all intents and purposes, radical environmentalists who would use any means necessary to take down corporations. As the board droned on, Bellow stared at a stone sculpture of what he supposed was the Hindu goddess Lakshmi, her many arms and legs reaching out to caress or destroy. He didn't give a damn who was behind the attacks as long as the source left itself open to him. It had been a long time. Right now he was itching to go, and he found the familiar focus reassuring—the way everything else just seemed to fade away from his peripheral vision. Another bug chaser he'd known a long time ago, when they were both young and hungry, had meditated just before a hunt. He'd described the feeling as finding the scratch on the head of a pin.

"I'll need complete access," Bellow interrupted, finally. "I know you've all got your own security issues and you won't want to give that up. But I want top-level clearance or I can't do my job."

There was silence. "Is that agreeable to everyone?" Crowther said. He looked frantic, concerned that

Bellow might say something even more outrageous.

They all looked blankly at him. A woman who may or may not have been over the age of forty said, "That simply isn't possible."

"There can't be any corners for it to hide in. If it has access, it will find the highest levels of security and hibernate."

"I don't understand," said the man with the pink, newborn face. "If this is a virus of some sort, it will have left corrupted files in its wake, and you can track it. But you talk like it's some kind of adaptable living thing."

"I believe it is capable of some independent thought. It may even be a human being. The fact is, we don't know what it looks like inside, or where it comes from, or why it's acting this way. Anyone who has witnessed this thing is dead."

"We've been able to trace some movement," Crowther said. "Three surges moving at a high rate of speed, attacking the main server in very sophisticated ways before flaming out. Won't that help?"

"That's like saying a program runs from code."

"Mr. Bellow," Pink-face said, "you're aware that New London is one of the largest, most diversified companies in the world. We have our hands in everything, from setting markets to silicone to consumer goods to space travel. We designed and built the city you're standing in, for God's sake, so you understand why we must be very careful. Ours is a fragile ecosystem,

24

Mr. Bellow, one that exists because we built and control it, but one that is finely balanced because the consumers—our customers—trust the New London brand. Our influences to that effect are subtle, and therefore transparent enough for the customers to be, for the most part, unaware of their existence. We simply cannot allow this illusion to break down. At the same time, we must also be very careful who we share our most top-level information with, for the same reasons."

"You've checked my references. You know I can be trusted, or I wouldn't be here."

Pink-face sighed. "There was some difference of opinion on that front. You've been out of the game for some time, haven't you? There are those of us who are worried it's been too long. But you received the majority vote, so here you are."

"I think what Mr. Au is trying to say," Crowther said, "is that we're concerned. We're all concerned, and rightly so. We simply cannot have any more of these incidents. The first two of them, because of the nature of the business, happened when the users were alone. This latest one was particularly...problematic because there was a witness."

"I want to talk to this person."

"I don't know if she's available," Crowther said. He looked around the table helplessly. "She's been detained."

"By your security, I'm sure," Bellow said. "So set up

a meeting. Look, someone—or something—is murdering your customers. I can probably stop it. But I can't do my job unless I have full access. No exceptions."

There was a long silence at the table. Beyond the glass wall, a Carrier swooped down from the black sky, its floodbeams flashing across the window and cutting off the city lights. "All right," the first woman said. "We'll give you access—if you sign the proper paperwork. Remember, we hold your body as collateral."

"How could I possibly forget? Now I'd like to ask you something."

"Go right ahead."

"Who created this system?"

The room fell into silence. The board members looked at each other. Pink-face cleared his throat. "That's none of your concern."

"I need to get an idea of the mind that built it. That will make it easier for me to sense anything unusual. Without laying the groundwork, I can't guarantee I'll be able to do what you ask."

"We're paying you a lot of money," the woman said. "You're supposed to be an expert."

"Is there a problem with meeting the programmer?"

"There are hundreds of programmers," she said. "We run a full-service facility here."

"But there must be someone in charge."

Pink-face frowned. "There is," he said, "but he values his privacy. It's rather unusual, actually. We ourselves don't even know his name. And he's terribly busy."

"All right, fine. At least give me access to saved versions of the early files."

"Why?"

"I want to feel this place being built."

Chapter 4

Checked into a New London Hilton cubicle downtown with his one bag of personal belongings stowed in the locker under the bed, Bellow slipped back out in search of information.

The streets of New London were hot and wet. A sulfur-laced fog had rolled in over the sea, making his eyes water and his stomach churn. He couldn't handle the humidity the way he did when he was young, when sweat was sweet and cleansing rather than something to shower off as quickly as possible.

On a nearby street corner, a small crowd had gathered. Someone was projecting a holographic signature into the fog, *The Transformation is coming,* along with the circle and arrow sign of the Church. The people were chanting something unintelligible. Above them rose a giant OLED billboard playing a clip of New London's latest virtual vacation, along with a voiceover speaking excitedly about the opportunities the New London Network offered those who were planning to get away for a while. "Bring your whole family," the soft female voice said. "Be transformed by all the comforts of a five star hotel and beach resort or a trip to the Venus moons for a spectacular sunset, all without leaving home."

Neon holographics painted the sky shades of red and green, and the New London virals flew at him with pinpoint precision, seductive stories that showed him what he could purchase if he wanted to be just like the latest holovid star. Underneath, he could feel the subtler waveforms pushing at his brain, trying to find their way in and alter his alphas. He'd always been able to feel them, unlike most of the general population, who didn't know when a thought in their heads was original and when it had been put there by someone else. Bellow supposed that was part of his talent, if one could call it that. To him, the whispering voices when he passed through a waveform zone were akin to sudden onset schizophrenia, and he wished to God the technology had never been invented.

The Carriers were quiet, their floodbeams off against the fog and guidance systems steering them low and fast around the tallest skyscrapers. Dogs slinked in and out of the shadows like ghosts, most of them strays with ribcages showing through patchwork skin.

He consulted with a web navigation system to get

his bearings and then blinked out again. The arcades were unusually empty. Bellow passed them without more than a glance, unable to face the flashing lights from game rooms, the kids with wires in their heads getting juiced like a bunch of goddamned lab experiments. Bellow knew what they said about him in the chat rooms: that he'd never really needed the hotsuit or corneal implants, that he was a natural net-sensitive. His abilities had made him legendary in some circles, but he had never seen himself the way others did. He didn't want to be anybody special. He just wanted to do his job and be left alone.

He took a right through Chinatown and reached a row of old-style English clubs complete with cobblestone streets. Inside the first was a band of Aerosmith clones. Projected above the heads of the crowd was a newsclip from the MSNetwork; the logo for New London Tower flashed and spun. A plump woman's ruined face blinked into view. Her hair had been nearly burned off, and the heat had made her flesh run liquid.

The latest victim, Stephie Vaille. Now the shit would hit the fan, Bellow thought. It would make what he had to do that much more difficult. He knew something about Vaille already from a records search, but wondered about the witness. Was it an employee, or someone who had been with her? His money was on a companion, since they had her locked down and the story had already broken on the news. An employee might have been kept completely quiet, but with a witness, they would have to release some information, no matter how bad it would get. Or was it possible that the press had managed to reach her already? If so, Bellow's job would be damn near impossible.

He took a table near the back, next to a couple of bodyguards with bands of grafted muscle across their backs and arms and a group of mutilants with artificially cleft palates and disease-enhanced skin. They looked at him as if he didn't fit in. A long time ago he'd had a girlfriend who'd looked at him like that. She'd decided to go in for elective surgery to remove her right breast, and he had been unable to talk her out of it. He was old fashioned. Preferred his women with two breasts. The last time he heard she was dancing in some high profile pheromone club that catered to fetishists. Go figure.

A woman approached him from the bar. She was tall and slender and wore a black, skintight bodysuit. She had the sort of unique looks plastic surgery couldn't fake: a round, cherubic face, nose a little too long, eyes wide apart and very dark; the symmetry of her features was off just enough to be intriguing. He'd seen her somewhere before and it unsettled him. He never forgot a face.

She slipped into the seat across from him. "I know you. You're the guy from New York, right? What do they call you, the Librarian? What are *you* doing here? Something to do with New London Tower?"

"Just a pleasure trip."

"That's a killer bug, you know? Nobody wants to use that wire anymore. Used to be some of the best gamers were on it. They gotta be getting somebody to go in. You'd be the guy if it were me."

"Sorry." He couldn't help staring at her familiar face, taken by the way she seemed utterly unaware of the effect she was having on the entire room full of men. Yet she knew plenty about the New London web scene. Maybe she just watched it on the news, like everyone else.

"So why do they call you the Librarian?"

"What?"

"Your hack name, silly. Where'd you get it?"

"The New York Exchange. I guess because I get in and out fast and quiet, and I know what I'm doing. I don't fuck around."

Hint of a smile. The light, musky scent of phero-mone perfume. Her tongue peeked out to wet full, pink lips. "'Seventeen seconds to glory?'"

It was what they'd started calling the NYE job after it was all over and the bug was dead. In the free net chat rooms he had become something of a celebrity in a star-starved world. Ever since the Hollywood crash there had been many digital heroes but few real ones. Big business sculpted and packaged everything with such precision it was difficult to tell where reality ended and dark marketing began.

"I suppose so. My fifteen minutes."

"So what happened to you, anyway?"

32

"I retired. It's a tough life, and I figured I could sleep late, build holograph projection kits in my basement, watch the races. Seemed like a good idea at the time."

"But you were so *good*—the Maui crash, everything..." She touched his bare forearm with her fingers, and it felt like an electric shock. He maintained his calm and managed not to jump, but only just. Lightly stroking his skin, she held his gaze with her own. "I watched you in the Vid-net. You were very nice-looking in that."

"It was a reconstruction. They smoothed my face and gave me a stronger jaw." Something was wrong here. If she knew so much about him, why didn't she know where his nickname came from?

"What's your name?"

"Kara."

And then it hit him, where he'd seen the face: in old movies, the two-dimensional kind blown across a flat screen. His father used to get drunk and watch them late at night in the basement.

"You're a clone. What'd they give you, sixteen years of memories? That's more than most get."

She removed her hand. His flesh tingled slightly where she'd touched him. "You don't have to be so awful about it. I was just being nice."

"Sure. Nice is good business. But I have to be honest, you're making me a little uncomfortable."

"And why is that?"

"You approach me at a bar. You're wearing an outfit that presents you as a sexual object. You're touching my arm within two minutes, and your perfume is specifically designed to arouse men. So far, so good, except you're asking me detailed questions about my life, which doesn't compute. If I were a john, you'd be quoting me prices right now."

Kara sat back and crossed her arms over her chest. Classic defensive posture, Bellow thought. Also didn't fit. God, but she was beautiful. What the hell was he doing here with her, anyway? He had a job to do, and he could begin down in the sewers, off the grid. As good as she looked, he didn't figure this woman was going to get him there.

"Excuse me for being impressed by your work."

"I'm not exactly the type of man you'd be interested in, now, am I? Again, assuming you're not looking for payment for your services."

"What sort of man do you picture me with, exactly?"

"One with money, for one thing. A sense of style and culture. Someone who knows his place in the world and goes after women like possessions to put on the shelf in his trophy room."

"Women as sexual experiences," Kara said. "Conquests. I think you have the wrong idea about me."

"I think you're lovely."

"And I fuck like a holovid star. Is that right? You think I'm a whore. It must be easier to go through life jumping to conclusions like that."

"In my line of work, you have to judge a situation quickly. If you don't, you might end up dead."

"I have all my shots," Kara said. "If that's what you're wondering."

But Bellow was no longer listening. Through the window he'd caught a glimpse of the same boy who had passed him on the way into New London Tower, the one with the tattoo. Something in the boy's face as he walked by...

Bellow was up and out of his chair before he had a chance to think. He heard the girl shout as he pushed past the bouncers at the door, then skidded left and pounded down the pavement, leaving the club's music behind. The boy was barely visible up ahead in the fog, black jacket trailing out behind him like a cape. He ducked into a vintage leather shop, Bellow close at his heels, and pushed through racks of musty smelling bomber jackets right out the back into a narrow alley where steam vents hissed and sputtered like angry machinery.

A door closed on Bellow's left with a slight click. It was short and squat, ebony metal, almost seamless within the soot-blackened brick. He blinked and pulled up an access grid. The door didn't show up on any web map. If he hadn't seen it swing shut, he would never have known it was there. Bellow had his wind up. New London wasn't as dangerous as some places he'd been, but there were plenty of spots to get in trouble. When he had been younger, he'd been able to handle himself just fine. But it had been a while since he'd been in a scrape, and his joints wouldn't work quite as well as they once had.

The handle had a thumbprint lock, but it was an old model and easy to bypass. In less than twenty seconds he had it open.

The corridor was lit with ancient tube fluorescents and crisscrossed by laser sentries. Bellow darted down the gritty tile, ignoring the beeps as the sentries armed themselves and centered on the small of his back. The corridor was too short for more than one shot. He counted silently to himself then darted quickly to the left as the charge released with a low pulse of sound. Light dug into the tile by his right arm, spitting up sparks as he skidded around the corner in time to see the boy slipping along the edge of a cavernous room filled with genetic equipment.

Tables with thermal-cyclers, gene extractors, Deep-well plates, tumblers, freeze dryers, and microscope cameras lined the walls next to full-size freezers coated in titanium. Containers filled with test tubes and sample jars sat behind a refrigeration unit with a tempered glass door. In another corner, a robotic arm slumped lifelessly over a deep steel sink and dissecting table, along with a professional holodeck imaging unit.

Bellow spotted a centrifugal concentrator floor unit and a top-of-the-line Tampo High-III Universal High-Throughput Screening System. Whoever owned this space was not messing around, he thought. The

equipment alone had to be worth millions.

But that was not what kept his attention. Vats filled with half-formed clones took up much of the central space. Genetic growth timelines had been tweaked; Bellow could almost see them expanding before his eyes.

Bubbles trickled to the surface. He heard a sound like water in a bathtub as one of the half-formed shapes twitched inside its vat of saline and blood, a bony limb ticking against glass.

Bellow saw a shadow move behind the vats, and he stepped forward. The boy did not try to run. He smiled as Bellow jacked him up against the vat.

"I told them to leave me alone. You go tell them again. No tails, understand? I do this my way or I'm gone."

The holographic hand on the boy's skull flexed like a spider crawling down his face. Bellow flinched and the boy twisted under his arm and darted away, his shadow bulging and oozing beyond the murky fluid tanks.

Bellow let him go. His interest had been caught by something else.

He stepped close to one of the tanks, a curious trembling in his stomach. There was a full-term clone inside. The shadow of a woman's naked breasts and curve of hips floated close, closer, and its features became visible. The eyes were closed, the nostrils not quite defined, but the looks were unmistakable.

Kara's sleeping face drifted down at him through smeared glass.

Chapter 5

His contact from Kong Nuantan's restaurant was small and lithe and spoke a broken Korean dialect that was hard to follow. He led Bellow back through the tiny dining area with its cheap plastic chairs, buffet line, and the smell of a damp basement into the narrow galley kitchen. Woks hissed and spit steam as the smell of ginger and scallions filled the air. The workers, Hispanic or Brazilian, all wore identical mesh uniforms with leggings underneath, their hair held back with nets. Several of them had prison holo-tattoos on their right wrists, the mark of the Jupiter moons.

At the back door, a second man emerged from the shadows and ran a hand along Bellow's body, pausing once near his right armpit. The man removed a tracking bug the size of a tick and squashed it between his fingers before it could nip and scrabble away. "One moment," the man said in English. He removed a pulse wand from his back pocket and switched it on. Bellow heard a sound like a hundred tiny marbles falling to the floor as the rest of the tracking bugs that had bred on his clothing went rigid, their navigation systems disrupted by the pulse, and tumbled from his body. He wondered who might have placed them on him: Crowther or maybe the boy while they were struggling among the vats.

It could have been any number of people, Bellow thought. There were very few places to hide from big business. He'd been sloppy, off his game. That worried him. The six years spent in retirement at the eco-pod in Arizona, partially shielded from the heat while cultured grasses grew in soft green carpets across golfing ranges and neatly manicured backyards, had softened him more than he realized. He didn't know why that had seemed like a good idea in the first place; manufactured suburbia had never been his thing. How had he spent his days, anyway? He had vague memories of a slow and painful recovery after Mexico City, making woodcraft projects in his basement and surfing vacation sites online through a drug-induced haze, but nothing concrete. It didn't seem possible that he could have survived.

The two men showed him out into a small alleyway where a manhole cover was ajar. Bellow pushed it the rest of the way aside and stepped down onto a rusted, dripping ladder, the rungs slimy with mold.

His senses were tingling as the two men set the

manhole cover back in place and he was plunged into darkness. This was not a frequently used entrance; his information was old.

He navigated down the rest of the way by feel, and at the bottom he lit a glow stick and stuck it in his front pocket. He was standing in about a foot of water at the entrance to a sewer line just big enough for him to walk through upright. It looked unused, and he wondered if he'd made a mistake. But then a light flashed at him from somewhere far ahead in the dripping darkness, and he set out through the muck, the sounds of tiny rodent feet skittering out of reach.

When he reached the end of the tunnel, the shadowy figure of a woman in dark clothing stepped out through a narrow gap in a series of rusted iron bars set into the wall. If he hadn't seen her emerge, he would have never imagined that a human being had passed that way in the last hundred years. She shined a flashlight in Bellow's face, blinding him. "Are you clean?"

"You already know I am from the sentries up top."

"Implants?"

"Corneal."

She glanced away and fumbled with something, and the light slipped down for just a moment. Bellow caught a glimpse of smooth, naked neck and soft hair. *I could have taken her out right there*, he thought. It was comforting to know he still recognized an opening.

She removed a device the size of a deck of cards from a battered blue backpack, the kind with double zippered pockets. Then the light was back in his face. He felt a momentary flash of heat as the wave disruptor did its work.

"You'll be offline for about two hours, no permanent damage," she said. She lowered the light and looked at him in the soft yellow glow; he saw jet-black hair and the same beautiful features from the bar.

"I don't believe it," Bellow said. "What the hell are *you* doing down here?"

"Did you think it was an accident, bumping into you like that?" Kara said, a smile gracing her lips. "Chin-Hae got your message. We had to make sure you weren't followed."

"But you *are* a clone."

"Recruited and officially offline," she said. "Been working with the resistance for a few months now. I was right behind you out of the club, but I lost you in the alley. Why were you chasing that kid, anyway?"

"Not sure," Bellow said. He thought about the half-formed shapes he'd seen in the vats, drifting among the blood and saline. He was again unsettled by how slow he'd been on the uptake; he'd let her get too close before without knowing her game. It wasn't like him, and he wondered if Mexico City had done permanent damage, after all. If so, this would be his last job, and it would surely end in a bad way.

He wondered, not for the first time, if this were some kind of test he didn't need to take, and whether he was like a washed-up ballplayer who wanted to return to some past glory but wasn't smart enough to know when his skills had eroded too far to get him there.

She reached out and touched his chest. "I meant what I said in that club, you know. You...fascinate me. I don't know why. I feel like I know you."

"You should be more careful who you meet in dark, lonely sewer pipes."

"You can't deny there's a connection. So what are we going to do about it?" The sexual energy flowing through her was almost unbearable. Her hand remained on his chest, and he could feel the heat of her touch through his clothes.

Maybe he'd misjudged her when they first met, or maybe not. One thing he did know was that he couldn't afford to get distracted.

He took a step back and her hand fell away. He felt a momentary ache at the look on her face. "Business," he said. "Before pleasure."

She studied his eyes a moment, then shrugged. "Did you bring something for him?"

He dug the motherboard out of his pocket. "It's not much. Late nineties, I think."

Kara took it in her hands and inspected it. "He'll be pleased."

She led the way back through the gap in the bars and into another tunnel. That led to another, then another. He saw no signs of human traffic in any of them. A few minutes later, they faced an ancient iron door with a spin lock—the kind that looked like it belonged on a submarine hatch. Kara turned it with little difficulty and the door swung open without a sound.

Beyond the door was a chamber made of old stone and concrete. Two men with portable directed energy weapons stood at attention about ten feet away. Bellow had been hit with one before and the pain had been nearly indescribable. Like cooking in his own skin. He showed them his palms.

"This really him?"

"He's okay," Kara said. "Stand down, Charlie."

They lowered their weapons. "Doesn't look like much," the other said. "Supposed to be some big deal bug hunter? What's the—"

Bellow was across the room in less than a second, disarming the one on the left with a soft Kali chop to the hand, careful not to break any bones, while removing the other's weapon with a gentle twist. It all happened so fast that nobody else had a chance to move.

The two men took a step back, mouths hanging open, the one called Charlie rubbing his wrist where Bellow had chopped him. Bellow smiled. He had worked hard on Filipino hand-to-hand combat practices when he was young, and he was glad to know he wasn't as rusty as he'd feared, at least not with this. The techniques came in handy often enough.

He had a feeling he was going to use them again very soon.

"Hey," Kara said. "You didn't have to do that.

Charlie, don't be such an ass. He's friendly."

"If these are the kind of resistance fighters Chin-Hae is recruiting, you're all in trouble," Bellow said.

"No harm, no foul," the one named Charlie said as Bellow handed the weapon back. He stepped away from the second door. "Sorry, dude."

This one was new steel with a fingerprint lock. Kara pressed the pad of her thumb to the lock, and it clicked open. A wash of voices hundreds strong hit Bellow in the face as the door opened, along with the ripe smell of many human bodies living in close proximity. Beyond lay a huge chamber teeming with life and divided clumsily into cubicles with cardboard and frosted plexiglass, tiny living quarters dotted with microwaves and couches and narrow cots.

Wash lines were strung up overhead, clothing hanging limply from them. Electric cords snaked everywhere through the dirt. A little boy with a dirt-smeared face peered out from behind an old cookstove, pointing a toy gun made of a plastic drawer handle and a rubber band at them.

"Cute," Bellow said.

"Abandoned subway switching station," Kara said. "Chin-Hae took it over from the homeless about two years ago and has been developing it ever since. Magnetically shielded from surveillance. Holds about four hundred, if you squeeze them in."

"Where's the power coming from?"

"They're tapping into New London's central artery.

The draw's so low compared to what they use, the company doesn't even notice."

A baby was crying somewhere out of sight as the boy shot a rubber band at them and ducked back behind the stove. "Quite an army," Bellow said. "When are you planning your coup?"

"Come on," Kara said. She led him down a winding passageway through the cubicles with Charlie and the other guard taking up the rear. Men and women stared at them as they passed; they left silence in their wake. By the time they reached the other side, the entire room had grown noticeably quieter, and most of the eyes were on them.

"They like you," Kara said. "They think you're closer to God."

"I'm just a hired gun. I go where the money is."

"Chin-Hae thinks highly of you."

"We go back a long way," Bellow said. "He owes me one. I'm about to collect."

Chapter 6

"William Bellow, after all this time. How good to see you, my friend." Chin-Hae stuck out his hand. "I'd get up, but you see it's become rather more difficult."

Bellow stepped into the crowded room and took Chin-Hae's slippery grip. He was a hugely fat man who wheeled himself around on a specially designed motorized chair, pale as a ghost from so many years without the sun, white rolls straining the sleeves of his shirt and pant seams. His head seemed to balance in a pocket of fat, and the smell of him was like old shoes left out in a rainstorm.

Still, he was a man of rare vision and talent. Too bad, Bellow thought, that his views had become so extreme they had tipped him over the edge and landed him down there, off the grid, one of the company's most wanted men. He was good enough to stay one step ahead of them for now, but they would get him eventually.

He took the board Bellow had brought and held it up to the light. "Hewlett Packard, 1998," he said. "Am I right?"

"I wouldn't bet against you."

"Ha. I'll use this, Will, and I thank you." He turned his chair to a pile of junked equipment in the corner and lifted a magnetic clip, which he attached to the board. To Bellow's left, a tower of computer casings had become a giant caterpillar weaving a cocoon made of yellow wires, and above it hung a graceful crane in flight, woven from hard drives and old DVDs. In another corner stood the sculpture of a man in full body armor made from theater speaker housings and receivers. Multi-colored wires peeked out like veins beneath a plastic shell of forearm muscle.

"You've been busy," Bellow said.

"This? Simply a form of meditation. My real passion is out there." Chin-Hae swept his arm toward a bank of computers and what lay beyond the wall. They were alone in a small room off the larger chamber, a room that might have once been a storage area or conductor's office. Through the thick metal door, Bellow heard the faint sounds of the people milling around. He wondered if Kara was among them.

"Do they know what you're trying to do?"

"Oh, yes." Chin-Hae nodded, rolls of fat jiggling in his neck. "This is all about the revolution, my friend. We spend many hours deprogramming those who find their way to us. New London has scrambled the minds of millions, but we can undo the damage."

"They're not much to look at."

"What can I do?" Chin-Hae held up his hands. "'Give me your tired, your poor, your huddled masses yearning to breathe free.' I can't turn them away if they're looking for the truth, and anyway it keeps them from Gutenberg's church. But there are warriors among them, make no mistake. Someday freedom will mean something again. We could use you, Will."

"I'm a mercenary."

"No." Chin-Hae shook his head. "You're an opportunist. There's opportunity here. Think of what we could accomplish with you fighting at our side! Think of the damage you could do to their networks from inside, with your talent. There's no one quite like you. The world would be changed forever."

"They have a security force of thousands and the best programmers in the world."

"They don't have me."

It might have sounded boastful, Bellow thought, if it weren't the truth. Chin-Hae had been New London's shining star many years ago, until he had begun to question their motives and methods. When they discovered he had started sabotaging the company with crippling viruses, Bellow was hired to undo the damage. He did so, but he also helped Chin-Hae escape, although New London had never suspected it.

A small yellow bird in a cage made a chirping sound, and Chin-Hae dipped his pudgy fingers into a

PRIME

painted china bowl on a desk and lifted seed through the bars. The bird hopped to his hand and ate rapidly, flicking husks with a violent twitch of its beak.

"My canary in a coal mine," he said, "in case they find us and choose to pump the sewers full of nerve gas. Now, do you mind? Just put this on for a moment, if you will. I'm sorry." He picked up a plastic helmet next to the china bowl and gave it to Bellow, who slipped it over his head. The plastic felt cool against his skin.

Chin-Hae engaged a holodeck from a slot on the desk, then began manipulating the wave signature settings that began to dance across its glowing surface. "Your name?" he said.

"William Bellow."

"You are how old?"

"Forty-three."

Chin-Hae studied the wave signatures for a moment, then tweaked a line with his pointer finger. "Do you know who I am?"

"Chin-Hae, former software developer and programmer for New London Industries. Leader of the Underground, artiste, and revolutionary."

"Tap the clip reader there, that's right." Chin-Hae sighed. "And your business here today?"

"I'm here to find out if you had anything to do with a series of electric pulses that have disrupted New London's network recently, resulting in the deaths of three users."

Chin-Hae's pudgy fingers paused for just a moment before resuming their activities across the holodeck. "Remarkable. Your waveforms seem completely unaffected by any dark marketing techniques. You are truly unique, Will. But you already know that."

"And I'm telling the truth."

Chin-Hae nodded. "It appears that way. Your alphas speak of honesty, and yet there is something unusual going on. Your brain signature doesn't match your stated age. If I didn't know better, I'd say you were a toddler."

"Young at heart," Bellow said. "Or in mind. Can we get on with it now?" He took off the helmet and handed it back. "Since when have you been recruiting clones?"

"You mean Kara? She's the first, as far as we know. The most sophisticated these days are nearly impossible to identify. She came to us not long ago—wanted to get out of the sex trade. She read sincere, and her wave patterns suggested an aptitude for our kind of work, so we welcomed her."

"I found vats of her in a warehouse not far from here."

Chin-Hae looked surprised. "Not ours. We don't engage in unnatural births. Our goal is antisprawl, as you know. Returning our Earth to her natural state. But once Pandora's box has been opened, it's difficult to close it again."

"Just be careful. New London's security force is everywhere, and those looking to Transform won't be too happy with you, either."

"If I didn't know any better, I'd say you were worried about me."

"We go back a long way."

"Indeed." Chin-Hae smiled. "Where have you been, Will? I heard you died on a job six years ago, fried up dark as toast. It was a great surprise and a true pleasure to hear from you yesterday."

"You never answered my question."

"What, the pulse deaths? No, we had nothing to do with that. Although I won't deny it's serving a purpose, waking up the population. New London Industries is as evil an entity as has ever existed on this planet—responsible for mass destruction of natural resources, support of organized crime, brainwashing countless citizens, the collapse of the polar ice caps. Now their answer is space colonization. Blast off and leave the mess behind. Have you heard that?"

"This latest victim, Stephanie Vaille," Bellow said. "Her father is one of yours."

"David is a valuable ally to the resistance, yes. I knew him way back when. He's gone dark now. I have no idea where he is."

"Killing his child with technology would make a point."

"We didn't do it," Chin-Hae said. "That's not our style, Will, and you know that. I'd be offended, but I know you're just doing your job."

"I believe you," Bellow said. "I need another favor."

"Name it."

"There was a witness to Stephanie's murder. I want to get at the security files, find out where this witness is and anything else I can about her."

"You can get all that yourself," Chin-Hae said. "Why come to me?"

"Because you're off the grid. Untraceable. I don't want them to know I'm looking. And I don't know who I can trust yet."

Chin-Hae chuckled again, rocking back in his chair. "Ain't that the truth, my friend. Hold on." He began to manipulate the data on the holodeck, his fingers a blur of motion.

"Do you ever find it strange," Bellow said as he watched Chin-Hae work, "that you've decided to devote the rest of your life to fighting technology, and yet here you are using it when it suits you and sculpting art from the refuse?"

Chin-Hae chuckled. "Technology is only a tool. It's the people who decide how to shape it. I used to believe that our perception was solid, that I could believe what my eyes saw, what my skin felt, and what my nose smelled. Now I know that isn't true. With the proper alterations you can smell a rose when it's really dog shit. I think people are like that. Don't you agree?"

"Not all of them."

"No," Chin-Hae said. "You, for example. You could pay to look twenty again. Fix that broken nose and rebuild your collagen. And yet you don't. Why?"

"I can't afford it."

"Come now. We both know you could if you made that a priority. I think perhaps you want to live as God made you. No hiding. You, William, are antisprawl in spite of your talent. Just like me." Chin-Hae let out a satisfied sigh. "Here we are. New London's security files. Your witness is a woman named Deborah Acevedo. She's a historian with Central Holdings, on vacation. Virtually inexperienced, very frightened. New London has her flagged as high risk: a potential maven whose alphas are not easily influenced. She's being kept in Tower security on level G. They're very worried about the damage she might do should they release her."

"And the victim's body?"

"Stephanie is being kept in the morgue under a security detail. I don't expect she'll get up and walk out. So who are they trying to keep from getting in, do you think?" Chin-Hae closed the holodeck abruptly. "That's all for now, I'm afraid. Can't stay online for too long or they'll lock in on me, regardless of my precautions. Is that enough for you?"

"Thank you, Chin-Hae."

"My pleasure. You come visit us anytime." The big man wheeled away from the desk and over to the birdcage where the little yellow canary sat with its head tucked under one wing. "I want to show you something, before you go."

He opened the cage door and wheeled himself back next to Bellow. They watched as the canary woke up and cocked its head, then hopped to the edge and peered out into the room. There was a moment of silence, pregnant with the possibilities. The bird fluttered its wings, and then hopped back to its perch.

"Cage them long enough, they don't know what freedom is anymore," Chin-Hae said softly. "You see?" He put a soft white hand on Bellow's arm, and when he looked up, his eyes were shining. "You might try to figure out what happened to you after Mexico City. I think it's important somehow. This retirement, was it voluntary? You were never one to sit idle for long."

Chapter 7

Back at his cubicle, Bellow stripped out of his sulfur-smelling clothes and slid into a vitamin shower. He was grimy with muck from the sewers and his whiskers had started growing again. He felt filthy inside and out.

After his shower he removed the OLED display he always carried from his valise and tacked it to the wall. He lay back on soft foam cushions and stared at an image of the night sky, huge and pregnant with stars. It never failed to calm him. The idea of the vastness of space while humanity was a mere speck on the screen kept him humble. He was nothing but an ant crawling through the earth, his pursuits to be forgotten instantly, their importance negligible compared to this.

When his heart rate had calmed to 50 beats per minute and his breathing was level and deep, he blinked into the web, crawl-scanning through thousands of files until he came to the one he wanted: movie stars from the twentieth century. He brought up a clip from one of Kara's Oscar-winning roles. It didn't matter what she did onscreen, he found himself studying her lips, her eyes, her delicate fingers as they held a cigarette. She was devastatingly beautiful, her mouth soft and sensual, her body smooth, tight, and rounded in all the right places. It made sense they would want to clone her, now that her rights had become public. Who wouldn't want to go to bed with a woman like that?

But who had done it? None of the usual suspects made much sense. Something nagged at him, and he didn't like the feeling. Perhaps he was spending too much time and energy trying to decipher her role in all of this. If her appearance in his life was random, then he was wasting time.

And yet it was to her that his mind kept drifting back, her face he could not dismiss.

A knock on his cubicle door, like an alarm clock jarring him from a dream.

He blinked out and focused on the ceiling, regaining his real-time balance. The walls seemed stiflingly close. At first he thought that the MSNetwork had found him, and he considered not answering at all, but when he opened the door it was Kara.

She pushed in past him and whirled. "Lock it."

"What do you want?"

"Just lock the fucking door!" She sat on his bed and put her hands to her face, her voice coming muffled through splayed fingers. "They're after me. They want to take me back in for brainwashing. They're saying

I'm a bad seed."

"You're off the grid and working for the resistance. I'd say that in their minds, that certainly qualifies. And while we're at it, who is 'they,' anyhow?"

She looked up at him. "My employers. Look, I don't want to go into this."

"You're in the sex trade. I understand."

"No." She shook her pretty head, glossy hair shimmering in the lights. "It's not what you think."

"How old are you, anyway?"

"Eighteen."

"But when were you incubated?"

"I don't know!"

A newborn clone of a twentieth century film star complete with teenage memories. No wonder she had joined the resistance. "How did you find me?"

"Chin-Hae checked the hotel records. He's happy to have me keep an eye on you, if you want to know the truth."

Bellow went to his door and peered through the peephole. That was all he needed, a visit from a couple of bio-pimps. As if he didn't have enough trouble keeping a low profile.

"You looked shocked to see me, underground. You could at least have apologized for the way you treated me in the club."

"I never said I was a gentleman."

You're so..." She made a frustrated sound. "All you originals are alike!"

59

"Listen," Bellow said, sitting next to her. "You're having adjustment problems, and that's perfectly natural. In your mind you've lived eighteen years, you've got eighteen years of memories of a life nothing at all like this one, and trying to figure all that out has got your head in a vice. You're a flesh and blood sex worker in a world that has started trying to convince everyone to go virtual to avoid pregnancies and venereal disease. So you've gone out on the lam and gotten yourself wrapped up in Chin-Hae's obsession as a way to find yourself. It's understandable."

"Don't be so smug," she said. "I don't know who I am or what I'm supposed to do, and neither do you. I just want people to treat me like a human being."

"We all want that. You're no different from the rest of the world."

"Aren't I?" Her chest hitched. The tears started rolling down her face.

Bellow put his arm around her shoulders. Even now he was conscious of her unbearable sexual energy. He felt like a miserable shit.

"You don't know what I've seen in those clubs," she said, swiping at her face with her sleeve. "What the human mind convinces itself is a good idea."

"Like mutilants?"

"There are those, sure. Funny name, not so funny results. Wounds created and torn apart so the scar gets worse. I've seen people begging to have their noses broken or earlobes removed, tongues split, toes or fingers amputated. But you know what really scares me? The ones who want to do it to someone else."

"There are drugs to handle that. Or alpha wave manipulators."

"These people don't want to be helped. They don't think it's a disease." She sniffled adorably. "I think it's an evolutionary kill switch gone haywire. You ever heard of caged mother rabbits that eat their young?"

"Jesus."

"They do. I'm not making this up. When they feel like they don't have enough space, they eat them. It's probably an instinct to protect the warren when resources get tight. I think that's what's going on with humans. Our self-destruct button's getting pushed, but people don't quite know what it means."

"How do you know about rabbits?"

"I read it somewhere. You know, they thought the world would be a perfect place by now. Look at *Transformations*: gene therapy to tweak disease, targeted drugs to change mood, wave manipulators to influence decisions, virtual reality to entertain us. So many people joining up every day, hoping for the miracle, their ascent into the new humanity. And yet here we are, still trying to kill each other and damaging ourselves in the process. Now we're spreading out in space. I wonder if we'll infect other planets, too."

"You've got a morbid imagination."

"—for a clone."

"I didn't mean that," Bellow said. "Look, I'm sorry.

You deserve more than I can give you. But I've got my mind on a job—"

"I *knew* it!" Kara said, pulling away all at once and staring excitely at him. "Chin-Hae wouldn't tell me, but you *are* here about the New London deaths! They hired you to go in, didn't they? You're going after the bug."

"I don't know what the hell you're talking about. New London's got a sim they want someone to test before they take it public, that's all."

"Bullshit. They're going to get buried if they don't fix this soon. You're the perfect guy." She stared at him, wide-eyed. "I can't believe it."

Bellow stood up and went to the OLED screen. He touched the pane and the scene changed from a sky full of sparkling stars to a cityscape at night. He heard her coming up behind him.

"At least tell me about it," she said softly. "What's it like to be inside like that? Do you see the code in your head? Or is it like some kind of telepathy?"

"I just...blank out. But another part of me is still there. And I start to feel what the machine is doing, what parts of it are right and what isn't supposed to be there. And I can feel where it's confused, or lost, or just different."

He turned to her and saw her eyes were closed. "I'm just a little more sensitive to it, that's all. It's nothing."

"No. *No.*" She opened her eyes and looked dreamily up at him. "Don't ever say that. People would kill to get what you have. People can get biochips implanted, but it's not the same. You're the closest thing to an actual transformation that anyone has ever seen. This is our chance to change for the better, to evolve into something more than we're capable of being alone. No, it's you, Will. You're it."

"How come you know so much about this if you're a newborn?"

"There's nothing wrong with being curious, is there?"

Curiosity killed the clone, Bellow thought, but didn't say anything. She was worked up enough as it was.

"Seems pretty strange that you're so interested in Gutenberg when you're involved with Chin-Hae's group. He doesn't exactly embrace the change."

"It's not that I'm interested in Gutenberg, exactly. I'm not a member of the church or anything. A lot of what he wrote is bullshit. I'm curious about part of the process he described, that's all. Becoming a different type of person. It's evolutionary."

"Sounds like splitting hairs, but okay."

"So what *did* happen to you, Will? It's like you've been erased. The last piece of data I could find ended six years ago. Can you at least tell me that?"

"There isn't much to it. I told you, I retired from the chase and hung around at home until I couldn't stand it anymore. I started thinking I'd get into managing for a while, looked into it. But owners get threatened by anyone who knows too much about what they're doing."

Owners had investments to protect, stock points that were sensitive to the slightest business tremor. Rumors of a power struggle could send the market listings tumbling. And Bellow didn't go in for hiding the truth.

"So why not own a wire yourself?"

He smiled. "It's not that easy." Although he *had* thought about it back then. He'd been young enough; he'd had all the experience and the money to show he was serious in attracting an investor or two. He'd even started planning a takeover, consulted with enough New Russian software experts to fill his head with smoke.

"So why did you retire, anyway?"

"I guess I lost my edge. Rumors spread over the web. Most owners wouldn't hire me anymore, and when they did I wandered around like a fighter after too many jabs to the face."

"But you're back now?"

He wasn't going to tell her about Mexico City. It was too long a road and the few memories he had retained were too frightening. Just thinking about it made the sweat trickle from under his arms.

"I guess so, if you want to call it that." He stared at her eyes and felt himself drowning in deep black pools. "You cut me up, the way you look at me. Clean through."

She smiled. "Does it hurt?"

"A little, but I can handle the pain."

"I wish you'd tell me more about New London. I want to know what you're going to do. God, I swear I've dreamed about you."

He didn't bother to deny anything more. She took both his hands in hers—warm, soft hands—and looked up into his face. "Now, are you going to fuck me or what?"

—§—

When he woke up the next morning, Kara was gone. He made sure nothing was missing, checked the hallway, sealed the door again and stumbled to the bathroom. He felt like he had a hangover, though he hadn't touched a drink the night before.

Jesus, she was something else. Newborn clones were like that, he'd heard, emotional swings to the extreme and fantastic in bed. True and true. She was soft and wet, eager to try anything, ferocious and hungry and loud. There was a vulnerability to her, an undercurrent of gentle shyness that was appealing. They had used each other's bodies as if they were long-lost lovers finally getting the chance to be together again. He just hoped she wouldn't go off telling everyone how she'd slept with New London's celebrity bug-killer.

There was something else about her, too, a depth he found astonishing in someone so young. The thing about the rabbit was disturbing, but showed a remarkable philosophical complexity. He wondered what else she might be capable of, given time.

And she was interested in his mission. Maybe too interested for her own good. What she'd said about him might be right, and he knew that back before Mexico City a lot of people in Gutenberg's new church had become obsessed with the idea that he would be the first to change. They'd even started stalking him on his off-hours, and his celebrity status had grown to the point of being uncomfortable. Once he'd found a woman hiding in his shower, and she'd refused to leave until he'd promised to return for her after his ascent.

The idea of all those people looking to him for guidance made Bellow break out in a cold sweat, and maybe that had had something to do with what had happened in Mexico City. He knew he was no savior. There were probably others out there already who could do much more than he had ever dreamed of doing. He'd heard rumors of children who had been virtually nursed through the network, who could code computers through thought, enter the web without any interface at all. Seen in that context, he was something of a dinosaur.

He blinked in and laid a misleading trail of false hits and identities to try to confuse anyone who might be watching, and then brought up what he could find on Stephanie Vaille. Her ID holograph showed a slightly overweight woman with an easy smile and bright, inquisitive eyes. She wore simple clothing and had an impressive list of degrees to her name, and she'd published a study on art in the new century two years before. He compared the vid capture of her blackened, ruined face and mapped the features to make sure it was her. The points matched. Then he dug deeper for information about her parents, but there was precious little other than what he'd already seen.

He probed at New London Tower's entry ports. Static broadcasts and infomercials; he hadn't paid the subscription fee. The server took him through a demonstration of endorphin rides, virtual vacation packages, gene surgeries, and implant options. He slipped through the smoke and probed deeper. The system became more sensitive to his requests for entry. He sensed an awakening, a series of responses gathering somewhere as the server spun another welcome sim that acquainted him with everything wonderful about New London Tower.

They were keeping him busy while they searched down his access code, which was still scrambled but not impossible to decipher. Security had been notified. If he was going to have a chance, he needed that clearance. And the board would only give it up if he were locked inside one of their cubicles.

Bellow blinked out and got into his hotsuit, the material adjusting temperature and clinging to his body like Lycra. He sensed fate coming hard down the track toward him, and he knew that it would find him whether he liked it or not. He had never been one of those people who could live a life blissfully clean and away from the underbelly of the world. He was once again at a crossroads: trust the company that had hired him and use what they gave him to get the job done if he could, or assume that everyone was an enemy until proven otherwise. He knew that his decision had already been made. He could feel himself on the edge of something big, a whirlpool swirling just beyond his feet, and he was about to get pulled in.

He threw on an overcoat and went down to New London Tower.

A reporter from the network was waiting. When she saw him she flicked on a spotlight and centered her remote camera unit. Wheels whirred across pavement, motors clicked into place. He could see himself holographically recreated inside the lens.

"We're streaming live on the web. Mr. Bellow, if I could speak with you a moment—"

"Fuck off." He shouldered past her, the light hot on the back of his neck.

She stayed with him. "You have to admit, Mr. Bellow, your appearance here is more than coincidence. New London has kept these deaths quiet long enough. Isn't it true that you've been hired to debug the New London server?"

He spun to face her. "Turn the camera off."

She looked at him eagerly, searching his expression for any hint of confession. "I can deal with that." The hotlight blinked out and the camera unit went limp.

"Now, what do you say? Tell me why they're going with you. I'll quote an unnamed source."

"I'm sure the building manager would be more than willing—"

"Fuck Crowther. I want the truth. We know about Mexico City, how you got lost inside and they had to send someone else in to drag you out. You spent how long—six months in rehab for that and years afterward off the map? They had to nanowash your synapses, isn't that true? There were rumors you died. You've never done another job."

"I had a little problem adjusting. Jet lag and all."

"It was a bit more than that. Mr. Bellow, we want to know what New London plans to do about the deaths of our city's citizens. Why would they hire a burned-out bug chaser to do such an important job? No offense."

"Anybody ever tell you you're a perfect case for gene manipulation?" When she opened her mouth again Bellow held up his hand. "One more word and you'll be fishing that remote unit out of your ass. Excuse me."

He left her standing there, mouth open, camera sagging at her side like a drunken old man who had fallen asleep at the bar.

Chapter 8

Deborah Acevedo was indeed in Tower Level G, behind a foot-thick pane of shatterproof glass in a room made to look like a vacation lounge rather than the prison cell it truly was. Bellow wondered whether anyone was ever fooled.

He watched her for a moment through the glass as she got up and poured herself a glass of water, then returned to sit at the table set up before the six-foot OLED screen that displayed a wash of bright, abstract colors sifting slowly back and forth like sea grass in the tide. The glass chirped and cooed as it tracked her movement. She was a plain, pleasant enough looking woman, but carried herself with slumped shoulders and shuffled gait. She would have been the perfect sidekick for a more vocal Stephanie Vaille.

He nodded at the two New London security officers, who stood with folded, meaty arms, watching him from behind mirrored monitor shields. Crowther had not been happy to grant him access to Level G, but he had grudgingly complied when Bellow had threatened to walk off the job. It seemed that the board had grown even more desperate in the hours since their meeting, and they were willing to give him everything he required. Until, of course, they weren't. This was the nature of boards. In Bellow's experience, the sudden reversal usually occurred at the worst possible time.

He told security to let him in, and one of them unlocked the door without a word, standing a little too close for an extra beat, an intimidation tactic that fell short although the man had close to three inches of height on Bellow. The New London forces were not exactly known for their subtlety.

Deborah looked up as he entered the room, and he saw weariness in her eyes and a glint of a deeper, more profound pain. She didn't look surprised to see him.

"I've told you people everything I know," she said. "Why don't you leave me alone?"

"I'm not 'you people,'" Bellow said. "As a matter of fact, I don't like them much, and they're not very happy I'm here to see you. I've got a job to do. I want to find out what killed your friend and put a stop to it before it happens again. Anything else is debris."

Deborah's eyes widened momentarily, and then she motioned to a chair. "Have a seat, Mr..."

"William Bellow."

"Mr. Bellow." Bellow sat down across from her. "What's your role here, exactly?"

"I'm a bug hunter."

"So you *do* work for New London."

"They're paying my fee, yes. But I couldn't care less about anything other than stopping these murders."

"Sounds pretty virtuous of you."

"Not really."

Deborah shook her head. She squeezed her eyes shut, and when she opened them again she was no longer completely there; a part of her, Bellow thought, was back in that room with her dead friend.

"Do you believe in karma, Mr. Bellow?"

"I think we make our own lives happen."

"I'm not much for religion. But maybe we're being punished for our sins. Virtual encounters, sexual relations with a machine. God wouldn't have wanted it this way. But our dear government does. The population explosion makes it easy to justify. No mess, no fuss, no children. What could be simpler?"

"Our government is getting paid under the table to endorse the concept. It's good for business."

Deborah's eyes focused on him abruptly. "You're right, of course. But where's the humanity? Where's the connection? The world we think we know doesn't exist, does it? It's all mind control now. Ninety-nine percent of the population has no clue what's going on under the surface. Hell, they're so blind they pay to get their minds fucked. If that's Gutenberg's idea of being Transformed, you can count me out."

"Those in the church would say you're just not trying hard enough."

"I wasn't. I hated it, you know, what we were doing. But I went along because of Stephie. I even suggested this very trip."

"What happened in there, Deborah?"

"I don't know, exactly. I came out and I smelled her...burning. She was on fire, jerking back and forth. I got up and tried to do something, but she was already gone."

"Can you think back on anything unusual that happened during your time inside—signs that something wasn't right—power surges, strange sounds, or disruptions in service?"

"Nothing." She shrugged. "When I came out and was holding my gear, I got some sort of shock, I remember that. Like static electricity when you walk across a rug, only a lot stronger."

"Did it burn you?"

"I tossed the gear before it could. You know what's funny? Stephie's parents spent most of their lives lecturing her about what's gone wrong with the world, warning her to keep away from anything she can't touch with her own two hands. They would be devastated by this. But I've been locked in here and I don't even know if they know she's dead, or how it happened."

"Stephanie's father is a member of the resistance."

She looked surprised. "How do you know that?"

"I have my sources."

"Stephie was his pride and joy. Not like her sister."

Bellow managed not to look too surprised, but she caught it anyway. "Oh, you didn't know about her twin? Neither side had recognized the relationship for years. Julia even had her name officially changed and the records wiped clean. She works for New London— or worked for them, anyway. I don't know where she is now. Stephie stopped talking about her a couple of years ago."

"Identical?"

"Stephie used to say that when they were kids, it was like looking in the mirror. They used to fool their friends all the time."

"What did she do for New London?"

"I'm not sure." Deborah drew in a breath. "You don't think—"

"You've been a big help," Bellow said, standing up. "I think we better end this now."

As he was halfway to the door, Deborah caught his arm. Her eyes were glittering as she pulled him close and spoke in his ear. "Stephie told me once that her sister was involved with a project called Prime."

"Never heard of it."

"I don't know what it means, but the way she said it, it seemed important. Mysterious, like she wasn't supposed to talk about it. I didn't tell anyone else about that. I don't trust them. Maybe you can find out more."

—§—

A quick check of records didn't turn up a reference to Julia Vaille, but then again, Bellow hadn't expected it to. If Julia was good at her job, she would have erased the trail. Nothing clicked on the name Prime either.

Nothing he could find in Stephanie Vaille's background would have made her anyone's target. Perhaps her death was simply a random event, as they'd been assuming all along. But it made him curious; someone, or something, targeting Julia Vaille and checking things like DNA signatures might, in the heat of the moment, make a mistake and take out her twin sister instead.

That only made him more curious about the two earlier deaths. Mark Beiser had been the first; he was described in the public record as retired. There was nothing about his earlier profession, but a check into classified files revealed that he had been on the books of a software development company called Blue Ribbon, which, Bellow discovered quickly enough, was a wholly owned subsidiary of New London Industries. There was nothing on file anywhere about the exact type of work he had done.

His wind up now, Bellow checked the second murder. Fernanda Rios was a geneticist working for a private lab specializing in gene therapy solutions to disease. No immediate connection, and at first he thought maybe he was looking down the wrong hole. But a flag on a citizenship database led him to a record of transactions occurring through overseas channels and behind closed doors, and through a series of dizzying switchbacks he found a reference to New London that could be a link.

Interesting. What exactly it all meant, he didn't know. But it seemed that there could be a lot more behind the scenes than New London was letting on.

It had been long enough, Bellow thought. Time to get back in the saddle.

He was going in.

—§—

The feeling of impending construction; a vast, skeletal presence lurking out of sight, feelers snaking out on all sides.

Bellow stood on the edge of a virtual wasteland of expectant space, listening to the rustling hiss of code coming to life. This was New London Tower exactly six months before it opened online, preserved forever in the saved files. At that time it had existed only inside the planning software, but soon it would be firmly planted in concrete. A web presence had been registered, and the address had already logged a million hits. He caught occasional glimpses of the digital faces of those passing through, curious users who could not wait, or those who had stumbled upon the construction site by chance.

New London Tower built its online presence even as its real walls were reaching up above the sand of

Southern Beach. He crawl-scanned through two months of records, watching the scene create itself in moments instead of days, feeling intersecting layers lay themselves like snakes upon one another, huge virtual walls climbing up into the sky.

He looked for anything unusual. If the original problem was bound in the underlying code, he could catch it here. A simple mistake could lead to a hole where a hacker could wriggle through, even an instability that could manifest itself much later as a full-fledged bug attack.

Whoever had built this place was no average programmer. Bridges and connections were being made that streamlined the server's duties, commands so perfectly imagined they were intuitive. Bellow scanned through another month before he began to see the beginnings of a functioning network. The server was logging fifty thousand hits an hour. Game rooms opened for business. Power grids glowed; data began to flow in streams of neon light. Somewhere deep inside the matrix, light pulsed like a heart. He slipped into a conduit and bled through rooms of coded floors and under firewalls. It was a static system, of course, all recorded, and it did not interact with him or even know he was there. He peeled away layers of data in search of the source of bright light.

Suddenly he found himself entangled in a dense web of code. He struggled to find his balance. His inputs were gone, everything empty, his eyes and ears and mouth filled with cotton. He fumbled blindly as bad memories began to close in, tried to reverse field in a world gone dark and silent.

Somewhere in the darkness, he felt the system stir and reach out for him.

He blinked back into the cool, static air of the private cubicle and focused on the wall, regaining his balance, his heart drumming. Something had sensed his presence. But that was impossible in a recorded datafile.

He blinked back in and crawled farther through the past, into an under-realized world of hatchwork and shadow. Something was coming at him through the fog. He sensed a multi-limbed creature moving at impossible speed; he blinked out again just as it reached his virtual presence.

Searing heat made him gasp. He smelled burning flesh and smoke, and looked down his arm at a blackened claw where his hand should have been.

Chapter 9

Bellow awoke inside a medical trauma unit. He flexed his fingers and felt the tingling of nerves as they reattached themselves and settled into place. Surgeons had removed his damaged hand at the wrist. Using cultivated stem cells from his body, they had teased gene paths, tweaked growth hormones, and grown him a new one on the back of a laboratory clone.

What the hell had happened in there? He'd never seen anything like that before. Someone—or something—had sensed him inside the recorded histories and come after him in a way that defied all logic. It had moved with a speed and agility he had only come close to seeing once before, at a time he'd rather not think about if he could help it.

Not exactly true, though, is it? The real truth was that he couldn't remember much of what had happened in Mexico City at all.

The door opened, and a medical technician entered

the room. "Glad to see you're back with us," he said. "Feeling okay?"

"If you call feeling like I've been run over by a Carrier okay, then yes."

The tech smiled. "Your hand was like a charcoal briquette. What happened anyway, did you reach into a rocket thruster or something?"

"Something like that."

"We've given you a quick body scan, and I have to say, you have the cells of a teenager. Remarkable. Deterioration of tendon and cartilage is minimal, and your telomerase are unusually long. Work done?"

"Does it look like I've had work done?"

"Hmmm. I suppose not. I'd say you were in your late forties except for the scan." He checked Bellow's new hand, tested muscle growth rates and responses to stimuli. "I'll leave you to rest now. You'll need to give your new hand a few hours to regain full strength. Try to stay in bed for a while. You might be in great shape, but nobody recovers from losing a limb in one day."

The tech left Bellow to the hum and hiss of machines. He drifted off and dreamed of floating helplessly through black cotton, eyes and ears and skin void of any feedback, as something came for him. The thing had many arms and legs and looked something like the goddess Lakshmi, and he had the feeling that whatever this thing was, it could open up and swallow the world.

Prime.

He woke up to a soft knock, the word still echoing

in his head. He opened his eyes, bathed in sweat and heart thumping, still half in the dream.

Kara slipped through the door. She looked beautiful. Something deep inside him was glad she'd come, and he didn't bother to question it.

She came over to the bed quickly, padding silently on the balls of her feet. "I had to see you," she whispered. "You've been set up."

"What the hell are you talking about? And how did you get in here without someone noticing?"

"Shhh. There's no time for any of that. Chin-Hae says they're listening. They've probably got this room bugged right now. We've got to get to a safe place."

"I'm not dressed."

"Hurry up, then. I'll help you." She got him to sit up and pull on his old hotsuit and overcoat, her long fingers lingering only a moment on his naked chest, then ducked her head into the hall. "It's clear. Come on." She pulled him through the door.

"Somebody else died last night," she said as she led him around the corner and down an empty flight of stairs to the next floor. "They say you're the one responsible. You'll be tried for murder."

He tried to shake off the cobwebs of anesthesia. "Hold on a minute—"

"There's no time," she said. She was nearly frantic. "Are you going to trust me or not?"

"Do I have a choice?"

—§—

The streets were wet with warm rain. Gutters steamed gently in the heavy air as Bellow and Kara slipped in and out of a sluggish crowd. He heard someone shout somewhere behind them, and Kara increased her pace until she was running.

Something was wrong, but he couldn't stop to think long enough to figure it out. His mind was still fuzzy from the drugs and whatever else they had done to him. He thought he probably should check for implanted chips, but Kara wouldn't stop long enough for him to do so.

They darted into an alley and through a dental surgeon's office, then back out through the emergency exit. More voices behind them.

"They're tracking us," she said. "Can you see them?"

He blinked into streaming datapaths and found three satellites turning to follow his infrared signature. Chin-Hae could handle things such as this. He placed a mental note in a drop box, put a flag up and exited back into the network. The satellites turned, turned...then began to swing the other way.

He ran a quick check on the latest death and found nothing. Maybe it hadn't been reported officially yet, but he found that strange.

He blinked back out. "Done."

"Not good enough," Kara said. She was leading him along the narrow, crowded streets of Chinatown, the smell of chicken and fish thick in the air. He recognized the area; the pub where he'd met her just a few nights before was ahead on their left.

Bellow's head was finally starting to clear, and he wanted some answers. He followed her down another street, through the familiar smells of the leather shop, and out the back door to the little alley with the hidden entrance. When she pressed the thumbprint lock and the door clicked open, he pulled her back.

"You keep showing up in the strangest places. Something I should know?"

"I'm just trying to help."

"Am I the rabbit, or are you?"

"Neither." She pulled down the edge of her Lycra shorts to show him a tiny pink scar on the inside of her hip. "See, my chip's gone. I'm off the grid, like I told you."

"What about the people chasing you yesterday?"

"We came to an understanding. I had Charlie and his friends talk to them."

"So the resistance is playing bodyguard now? Good to know."

"Charlie's a little sweet on me. He's just trying to help." She put a hand up to his lips. "You and me, we're the same. Trying to escape."

"I don't even know what I'm running from."

"New London is planting rumors that you've been hacking into their server and killing those people. They're saying it's all a scheme so you can ride in and save the day, regain your celebrity status. Don't you get it? They need someone to take the blame. Why do you think they replaced your hand?"

Sounds from the street, running footsteps. Kara swung open the door. "Come on."

Bellow ducked into darkness. The hallway he remembered was empty. He listened for the laser sentries and heard nothing. Kara was already disappearing around the corner.

He followed quietly, his senses on edge. A dim glow came from the room where the vats were kept. He slipped around the wall and moved farther down to an area of the room he had hadn't seen before and faced the vague forms floating in bloody fluid. Far above him, the arched beams of the ceiling blended into shadow. Kara had vanished. He took a step closer and touched a finger to damp glass. Blinked into the web, searched through layers of data for the blueprints to this building. The space on the grid was nothing but a black, empty hole.

He blinked out again as a shadowy figure twitched inside the closest vat, and the face of the clone floated gently through the fluid and came into focus.

This one was almost fully formed. Bellow stumbled away from the milky, lifeless eyes and familiar line of the jaw, a terrible churning in his belly.

He was still trying to make sense of this new development when Kara screamed from somewhere deeper inside the building and two shadows approached from between the hulking vats to his left.

The boy from New London Tower and a twin. More clones.

"Howdy, folks," Bellow said. He showed his open palms in a gesture of friendliness. "That looks an awful lot like me in there. Somebody want to tell me what's going on?"

The two clones looked at each other. "Sorry," one of them said. "But you're in over your head."

"Where the hell am I? Can you tell me that?"

"A private incubating room," the other clone said. "It's ours, because we like ourselves. We're the only ones we trust."

"Seems to limit your options quite a bit," Bellow said. "What about Kara? She one of yours too?"

"She's lost focus. She needs to be brought back in line."

"What have you done with her?"

"Enough questions." One of the clones launched himself at Bellow and he slipped sideways, but then someone had wrapped arms around him from behind and the other came at him again.

Bellow twisted upward and pushed off the approaching clone's chest with his feet, flipping up and over, twisting hard with his arms as he did so. He heard a bone snap as the clone holding him fell hard onto concrete. He thrust an elbow backward, felt it connect with something soft, and rolled off and away. The second clone had regained his feet and held a laser blade in his hand. The cutting end flashed red before

Bellow was on him with a rage that burned up through his stomach and out through a vicious chop to the wrist and throat.

The clone dropped without a sound, the laser blade clattering to the floor. Bellow reached to pick it up and turned to face the other one, but he was already vanishing around the shadowy vats at the far end of the room.

Enough fucking around, Bellow thought. *What the hell is going on?* They had copies of *him* growing in there. He thumbed the kill switch on the blade and stuck it into the pocket of his overcoat, then ducked around the vats, listening carefully for any sound.

Kara had screamed. He thought of the clones and what they might do to bring her back in line, and he thought he might be sick. He reached the far wall and found another door, which led into a narrow metal staircase leading down.

Bellow scanned the darkness below and then went in low and fast, stopping once on a landing halfway down to make sure the rest was secure. At the bottom was a concrete-floored basement room full of old props for some kind of theater: a backdrop painted to look like barren trees in the winter, wardrobes of dusty old costumes in bright colors, and a broken unicycle leaning in a corner.

A life-sized clown holding balloons stood alone, draped with a sheer burgundy cloth; it took a moment for Bellow to realize it was a statue and that the balloons were painted plywood.

In the center of the floor was a drainage grate left partially ajar. He slid it aside to reveal a ladder going down into darkness and the smell of earth and wet rock.

Chapter 10

Back down, into the sewers.

There were lights every ten feet, dim bare bulbs behind metal cages built into the low ceiling. This section of the tunnel was older and it looked like a medieval torture dungeon with its rough-hewn stone and ancient stained brick. This was all that was left of the old London after the structures above ground had begun to crumble in the constant rain and heat and then been razed to the ground by New London's giant automated building machines. A city of centuries gone in less than a year, and a new one growing up like magic in its place.

Bellow checked himself over as he jogged down the passageway, testing his new hand and finding it sufficiently up to speed. He searched his body carefully for any sign they had implanted a tracking chip or subcutaneous slow release drug. He found nothing sore or swollen. There was no time to look for breeders; he'd just have to hope he was clean.

He'd noticed from the condition of the ladder's rungs that someone had descended recently, and there were fresh footprints in the muck at the base of the first tunnel. They turned right at the first junction, then he lost them when the floor turned into six inches of slow-trickling, brackish water.

By then it didn't matter—he could hear them.

He followed at a safe distance, far enough away to keep anyone from knowing he was there, but close enough not to lose the clones. They didn't talk much— or at least he couldn't make out anything they were saying—but he heard their footsteps. They weren't trying to remain quiet; maybe they thought he wouldn't come down after them.

Or maybe they didn't care. Bellow was itching to break into a run, but he held back. If they had Kara, they might hurt her before he could stop them unless he used the element of surprise.

And if they don't have her?

When he realized how important she had become to him, he almost turned back. A feeling like that was deadly. He couldn't afford to have any point of weakness, and she was a big one.

You've only known her for a couple of days, he told himself. *That's crazy. It can't be what you think. You can't be in love with her.*

The ache in his chest when he imagined not seeing

her again told him otherwise.

The tunnel joined a larger central artery and the series of bulbs in cages above his head ended. The clones were using their own light. He followed the faint glow ahead to a familiar set of broken iron bars.

Chin-Hae.

Bellow stood in the quickly spreading darkness and considered what that meant.

The glow from the space beyond the bars was fading swiftly. He had to move or risk lighting a glow stick and giving himself away. He wasn't easily frightened, but the idea of stumbling around alone down in the pitch black was not an option. He stepped through the bars and into darkness, and once he'd become satisfied that the clones were gone and he was alone, he lit a glow stick and kept it cupped behind his hands, releasing a few beams of light.

The way was familiar to him, and he navigated through the remaining tunnels until he reached the iron door with the ancient spin lock. It was partially ajar.

This had the appearance of a trap. Appearances could be deceiving, Bellow reminded himself, but in his experience it was far better to be cautious. And yet, what choice did he have? Return to the surface and leave Kara behind? He couldn't bear the thought of it, and he had never been one to back down from a challenge.

If he was going down, he would do it fighting.

Bellow swung the door open and stepped inside.

Chapter 11

The small room was empty.

He held up the glow stick. The light reflected back nothing but bare stone. No Charlie and his friend with weapons, no clones. No Kara. The newer steel door on the other side was also partially open, and he pushed through into the huge chamber.

Here were the people. It was like walking into the middle of a whispered private conversation. All voices stopped, and he felt hundreds of eyes on him from the main alleyway through the maze. The feeling in the air was different this time; heads ducked back into cubicles and out of the way as he passed; people hid from him as if he were someone to fear.

He found Chin-Hae alone in his office. The big man didn't seem surprised to see him, but Bellow noticed the thin sheen of sweat on his skin, the way his eyes showed more white than usual, and the shallow, fast pace of his breathing.

"The Librarian, twice in one week? This is an unexpected pleasure."

"Where is she, Chin-Hae?"

"Not here." The man shook his head, and wattles of flesh below his chin jiggled in time. "You really should leave. It isn't safe for you."

"Is that a threat?"

"I would never threaten you, my friend. I value my life far too much."

"Then I'll say it again; I know they came in here, and I know they have her with them. Where is she?"

"Oh, Will, you've gotten into something now, haven't you?

"Look at yourself. You've lost focus completely, worried to death over a woman who isn't worth your time. She's a clone, and a traitor to boot, and if she doesn't belong to us and she's not a sex worker, then who does she work for?"

"I don't know."

"What you really should be thinking about is Prime."

"That's the second time today I've heard that name. The people being killed, they were a part of it, weren't they?"

"It does seem that way. I wish I had all the answers. But I'm not God, and I haven't Transformed, as they say. We all want to become something else— something better—don't we? Everyone has a wish they want granted."

"Stop talking in riddles."

"But I'm speaking quite plainly. That's the key, don't you see? Humankind's greatest weakness. The wish to become someone else can be exploited. Who do you think Gutenberg really is, and why did he create the Transformations movement? What was his purpose—goodwill toward man? My time is running short, I'm afraid, but you should understand that the world is at a refraction point. Nothing is going to be the same after this—for any of you. I wish I could be there to see it."

"You'll survive. You always do."

Chin-Hae's eyes were gleaming, his words coming faster. "Listen to me now, Will. The answers you're looking for can be found in only one place, somewhere within New London Industries, but you must be careful—"

A noise from behind made Bellow whirl. The two clones and six members of the New London Security Force had come into the room. The clones had Kara between them. Her mouth had been taped shut, her hands secured behind her back.

Kara's eyes were wide and frightened as they scanned the room for him, then settled on his face. She shook her head frantically, making choking sounds from behind the tape.

The security team held Hammer Glock 1800 full automatics with high-capacity magazines, modified for rapid fire. No directed energy weapons there; these were meant for killing. The men fanned out across the room, surrounding Bellow and Chin-Hae with careful precision.

"They came about an hour ago," Chin-Hae said sadly. "Tracked you to me, or perhaps she brought them in." He inclined his head in Kara's direction. "I'm sorry, I had no choice. I couldn't warn you. This is bigger than either of us. They threatened to set off a pulse bomb and kill everyone in the chamber."

"Enough of the talk," said one of the clones holding Kara. "We're here to bring you back to the surface."

"And then what?"

"We want you to finish the job you started."

"Let her go, and I'll come willingly. Don't, and you're going to get hurt."

The security team glanced at each other. One of them chuckled. "There are eight of us, and we're armed," he said. "What the hell are you going to do?"

There was more scattered laughter, but Bellow sensed a tension underneath it. They knew who he was, and maybe something of what he might do. They would be tight, their trigger fingers itchy. He might be able to use that to his advantage.

"So you're all working for New London?" he said, edging casually toward the closest member of the security team, the one who had spoken. "Is that it? Kara too?"

"She's a useless bitch," the first clone said.

"We're going to have to shut her down," the other

clone said. "We thought you might like to watch. It will remind you who is in charge."

He pulled a large laser blade from a case on his belt and flicked it on. The edge glowed a deadly red.

"Easy," Bellow said. "Nobody has to get hurt."

The clone smiled at him. Then he turned, and with one swift movement, he slit Kara's throat.

A gout of thick blood splashed to the floor as Kara's eyes rolled back in her head and her knees buckled.

She slumped. Her body, half held up by the clones, started to shudder.

Bellow felt the world tremble beneath his feet. Panic electrified him as he reached impotently for her from across the room. She was too far away, the wound was too deep, the blood coming too fast. There was nothing he could do.

No. Nothing made any sense to him anymore—who he was, or what he was meant to accomplish, or how this woman had so completely overwhelmed his emotions in such a short time. He could not think of how this had come to pass.

She was dying before his eyes, and he could not reach her fast enough to save her.

The closest guard brought up his gun. A terrible, mind-altering rage swept Bellow up in a crashing wave that pushed everything else aside. His senses shrank to a single, focused point. With one lightning-quick move, he pulled the laser blade he'd taken earlier from the clone out of the pocket of his coat, flicked on the blade and swept it upward under the guard's wrist, shearing muscle and bone clean through.

Time slowed down until it became a series of stuttering snapshots. The guard's severed hand with the gun flew upward, finger tightening reflexively on the trigger and letting loose a hail of bullets that ripped through the room, tearing through Chin-Hae's sculpture of the man in armor and shredding it into a hundred pieces of shattered plastic and silicone. Bellow released the laser blade, grabbed the hand and gun from midair, and turned with it still firing as he felt the warm blood from the guard's wrist stump spatter his back.

He aimed high as he spun in a circle, spraying the room with angry, whining hornets that took out the five other guards' faces in an explosion of blood and bone and drove the two clones backward against the door, where they slid into a limp heap on the floor.

It was over in less than three seconds. Nobody else had had the time to get off a single shot. He was left in a dripping, cordite-filled silence, broken only by Chin-Hae's labored wheeze. Bellow's aim had sent the slugs just over the fat man's head as he sat in his chair, and now he lay half-reclined in quivering terror, one huge hand clutching at his chest.

The terrible silence settled like a lead weight over them, pushing down on Bellow's shoulders with the strength of a colossus, driving him down toward the floor. He saw it in the chipped concrete walls, the screens that had gone suddenly dark in the angry swarm of bullets, the blood that had spattered everywhere and ran freely like a red ocean toward his feet.

The guard with the severed hand was holding his wrist and moaning. Bellow walked over and put one bullet between his eyes. Everyone else lay motionless. Kara had slipped to the floor when the clones had released her, and she lay facedown in a pool of her own blood.

He turned her gently and winced at the deep slice in her neck. Her carotid artery had been severed. She was already gone, the glint in her lovely eyes faded to a dull and vacant haze.

He stood up again, the rage alive and screaming within him, burning a hole through the center of his being. He walked back over to where Chin-Hae lay half-reclined in his chair.

The smell of urine was sharp in the air. Bellow took him by his fat throat. "What is Prime?" he said, leaning close into the man's face.

"I...don't...know for sure," Chin-Hae whispered. "Something top secret...a group of three programmers and two scientists working for New London at the very highest level. Please. You're hurting me."

Bellow released him. "Julia Vaille is one of them. Stephanie Vaille's twin sister. But she changed her name."

"I don't know what she calls herself now. All the records have been purged. The rumor was that New

London got their hands on something special. Nobody knew what it was, but suddenly their software began to change. It was better than before, way better. Better, even, than I could do."

"This had something to do with the Prime group?"

"I don't know."

There was a noise near the door. One of the guards was executing a jerking, one-armed crawl, the back of his head a bloody red mess. Bellow put a bullet in the man's spine and turned back.

"Please believe me," Chin-Hae said. "I had no choice. They came in fast and overwhelmed my guards. There are more of them coming. You'll never get past them."

"Don't bet on it," Bellow said.

"You saved my life again."

"Your reprieve may be short. Before she was taken, Kara told me someone else died last night, another member of the group. She also told me I was being set up."

Chin-Hae struggled to sit up in his chair. "I know nothing about this, I swear. I would have heard of another death through my sources."

"Who are the others involved in Prime?"

"A man named Mark Beiser, a programmer; he was the first to die. And two other women. Fernanda Rios, a geneticist. She's dead too. And Mo Naam—those are the names I know. They've gone dark and deep underground, off the grid. They're running from someone, or something."

The canary fluttered in its cage, beating its wings against the bars. Feathers drifted into the air as it flew back and forth, pecking and swooping.

"You must go now, before it's too late," Chin-Hae said. "There's only one place to find your answers. Ask them about Gutenberg. Ask them why they brought you in, Will. It's a question that's been bothering me from the start. There are other bug killers. Why you?"

Bellow left Chin-Hae and stepped to the door. He did not look at Kara's body on the floor, her face grown pale and bloodless in death, her chest forever still. He would use his anger to paint his soul black. He had only one purpose now.

Chin-Hae might know more than he let on, but he wasn't going to tell Bellow. Whatever was going on, the true answers could be found at New London Tower. It was time to cut through the bullshit and get his hands around this thing's neck.

He only hoped that when he got there he wouldn't hesitate long enough for it to make a difference.

Chapter 12

When Bellow walked through the front doors, the manager looked as though he'd seen a ghost. "I understood you were in the hospital," he said, hurrying to keep up as Bellow kept walking. "A terrible thing, what happened to your hand—good lord, the blood!" He motioned to Bellow's coat. "Is it yours?"

"Unfortunately, no."

"What have you done?"

"I'm guessing you probably heard already."

"I don't know what you mean. How would I—"

"Cut the bullshit, Crowther. You've been tracking me, and you sent the clones and your little security force to bring me back. I don't take kindly to being used, and I don't like being manhandled. They're all dead now. Better send a cleanup crew."

Crowther flipped a hand at the sentries who began to close in on them, and they backed away quickly.

"What are you doing here?"

"I'm going in. From a cubicle. Strap on the monitors, hold my body hostage, do whatever you need to do. That's what you wanted, isn't it?"

"I'm not sure this is the right time."

"What's not to like? Beautiful evening, the net's quiet, love is in the air." Bellow stopped suddenly and turned to face the building manager. "What are you afraid of, anyway? We're wasting time. Let's get it on."

Perhaps his eyes were a little too frantic. For a moment he thought the man might actually say no. But then Crowther sighed and nodded. "All right, if that's what you want. I wouldn't recommend it after what happened earlier to your hand. It's too dangerous. But I won't stop you."

They stepped into the elevator and rode up in awkward silence. Bellow ignored the news broadcast playing in high definition three-dimensional glory across the translucent doors, at least until he saw his own face once again. It was a motion capture of himself from after the Mexico City debacle. His cheeks were plump enough, almost boyish, but his eyes held a haunted look that spoke of more years and sorrows than he cared to count.

For a moment something important seemed to be within his grasp, but it slipped away and he was left with the frustrating feeling that he remained one step behind everyone else.

"The media is looking for you," the manager said,

almost shyly. "We've tried to keep them off the scent until now, but we can't do that forever. You seem to have upset them."

Bellow turned away to keep from grimacing. "Some people are just unlucky. Haven't you paid them off by now?"

"Regardless of what some people might think, the MSNetwork operates as an independent entity from New London Industries. We'd very much like to control their actions, to be honest, but it doesn't work that way."

"If you say so." Bellow again resisted the urge to grab Crowther by the throat and throw him against the elevator wall. Maybe he knew about the clones and what Bellow had done to them, or maybe he was just a pawn for the board, or for someone else. The Prime group came to mind; who were they, and why were they being targeted for death?

He thought about asking Crowther, but decided it was too risky. There were too many loose ends, and something was barking at him to watch his back. The less said, the better.

He flashed back to the blood and smoke of the earlier shootout and Kara lying dead on the floor. His mind was spinning and he felt like he was on the edge of losing control completely. Was he being set up, as she'd told him? If so, by whom? New London Tower didn't make sense—they had too much to lose here.

—§—

Crowther showed him the inside of the same empty cubicle where he'd burned his hand. "If you need anything," he said, "just call."

"Did someone else die last night, Crowther?"

Crowther looked confused. "There were no incidents, other than your hand, of course. Why?"

"I'd heard a rumor, but couldn't confirm anything through the net. Just wanted to make sure."

Crowther nodded once, and then left. Kara had lied to him. Why? To get him out of the medical unit more quickly? It seemed like as good an answer as any.

Bellow knew they would be watching closely through the monitors. He wasted no time in stripping off his coat and hanging the bloodstained garment in the corner; he did not leave his hotsuit on, either. He didn't need it. He would ride this one the way he'd been born, sliding in and out on his own slippery flesh. The world buzzed before him like a fluorescent light, and he knew he was as tuned in as he had ever been in his life. He felt Kara's presence, and along with it came the anger that pushed him forward; he welcomed it because it left no room for anything else.

He lay back in the zero gravity pod and everything faded to a soft, cool green. The walls and slightly arched ceiling overhead were perfectly smooth and empty. He blinked in, located a port of access and a programmer's backdoor, and slipped below the interface meant for everyone else as effortlessly as a knife through softened butter.

There were users on the other side of the port, and he watched them as though through a one-way peep-hole. Three women played the virtual slots in a private casino room; their tab was rising, and he could see in a blink that their funding account was running dry. The bank had probably set a limit and they would play until it was gone, but they were strictly recreational users. New London's alpha waveforms were hard at work, pushing the urge to bet more and to take more risks, and the women were eating them up. Tomorrow they would wake up with virtual hangovers and a hollow feeling inside and wonder why they had gone so far...until their alphas were tweaked again for some other purpose.

This was the rest of the world, always searching for something to fill the emptiness inside. Chin-Hae was right.

Within moments he could find out where they lived, what their families were like, their financial background, the kind of vehicles they drove, prescriptions they took, even peek at their medical records and sexual histories. He could find out whether they were members of the Church of Transformations.

A sour taste filled his mouth, and he set himself adrift into the main data stream.

The building was an enormous physical and virtual space, much more complete and powerful than it had been in the early files. Millions of users across the globe were running software, and the building handled them all seamlessly and with little effort. It breathed deeply and evenly like a body in a meditative state, power flowing up from below and coursing out through countless lines like veins feeding blood to the skin. He did not sense a single corrupted file or unnecessary loop. It did not seem possible that anyone could have created such a thing.

Bellow probed gently through various ports until a higher-level security access prompt brought him up short, but his signature was recognized and he was let through without trouble. They were letting him go, then. Crowther either hadn't told the board about his little massacre in the sewers or they didn't care.

He could sense streams of data running everywhere; these were the private files and programs where the real money was made. He saw why the board had wanted to keep him out: a lively slave pornography trade exchange in real time; a network of pirated software running on mirrored servers; money-laundering efforts concealed beneath complex webs of false data, empty rooms, and dead-end code. It was illegal as hell, but it wasn't what he was looking for, and nothing else was hiding there.

A bug would set off waves inside the net, and to find one he had to get up close and personal with that code. He had to listen. Binary was like any other language; it could be learned by anyone who was patient and had a knack for linguistics. He backed out and tried to track down any broken fragments and corruption that would signal that something foreign had gone through.

Bellow was concentrating so hard that he almost missed it. Intent on finding gibberish and broken lines, searching for an increase in traffic, a hotbed of activity and confusion, he overlooked the opposite. Beyond the normal streams and a series of partitions there was something that felt like a black hole. He could sense nothing, feel nothing coming from it, would not even have known that it was there save for the subtle influence it had on the surrounding code.

As he moved in that direction he sensed another presence turn his way, and this one was hot. It struck with a speed and precision that made him gasp, hurtling up a data stream like a spider skittering along a web. He leapt to another line as it burned past him, the surge of energy like a lightning bolt, and then he was off in a frantic game of cat and mouse, twisting and turning and leaping from stream to stream, ports flashing by like twinkling lights in an everlasting nightscape. The streams blurred into quicksilver as he used every trick he had to stay one millisecond ahead. But he was older now, and rusty, and no match for something like this. It was gaining too quickly.

He ducked under a firewall using the highest access code he had and shut it all down into blackness, detaching himself like a climber from a clip and harness.

He had to catch his breath, had to figure out why this thing was chasing him. For a long moment there was nothing but utter silence. This deep inside he could hear and feel nothing. Not his heartbeat in his ears or the sound of his own breathing.

Bellow felt the old familiar panic creeping up on him, the way it had felt in Mexico City, weightless and set adrift within himself until nothing else existed but his own mind, and eventually not even that. He tried to remember the job and found a black hole inside himself just like the one he had found in the code; an absence of clear memory that was as frustrating as it was surprising. How could anyone forget what it was like to hover on the edge of death? And yet he had. It was as if someone had come along with a scalpel and neatly removed that cluster of neurons, leaving a scar that had saved his life but erased the experience from his memory forever.

He hadn't wanted to think about Mexico City or what it had meant. Instead, he had buried his head in the sand, and that decision had cost him dearly. If he had taken the time to understand himself and his own limitations, would Kara still be alive?

The night was no longer black and empty. He felt something coming.

The power surge was like a quickly building static charge, buzzing and hissing like a live wire that had snapped in two. He punched out and back into the web as his hiding place lit up like a supernova.

PRIME

The results were catastrophic, ripping programs to shreds, snapping lines of corrupted files across the net like the tails of snakes. Bellow turned and ran, but the spider followed him across vast distances of dense code. His instinct led him straight to the black hole, searching for shelter, for anything but this open expanse of infinite space. As he approached, he reached out and felt for a trapdoor and threw his access codes at it with everything he had, praying for a miracle.

Chapter 13

Bellow rolled across soft sand. He struggled to orient himself. Somehow he'd come through the back end and dropped right into a simulation's waiting lap. He braced for the sudden surge of light and power as the bug hit and tore the sim to shreds, but it didn't come.

Curious, he stood up, sand shifting under his bare feet. It sparkled in light-rainbow hues, every grain sharply defined and unique. He watched his toes sink into the heat as the sand closed over their tops, sticking to his skin.

He could smell seawater and salt flats.

Before him stretched an endless beach. To his right were high dunes with scattered grass rippling in the breeze. To his left, waves lapped against the shore and an ocean stretched out to the horizon line, a flat, silver, blank screen.

An infant world that had yet to fill out. Even so, the

detail in the sim was breathtaking. He watched the waves break against the sand, grains swirling and ebbing with the pull of the tide; he walked to the water's edge and crouched, cupping cold salt water and letting it run through his fingers. The illusion was seamless. Bellow shivered, aware of a presence other than his own.

When he stood up again a boy was sitting about ten feet away. He sat facing the sea, digging with a yellow plastic shovel. He was no older than six or seven, slightly pudgy with sun-bleached hair and wearing light nylon swimming shorts.

Bellow walked over and the boy turned to look up at him. His pupils were the flat silver color of the horizon.

"We're sorry about the sentry," the boy said. His mouth did not move but his voice was louder than the hissing surf.

"You're the real bug," Bellow said. "That was just a decoy, a trip wire. Damn good one, too. I'm impressed."

The boy didn't answer. He began to pack sand into a green pail shaped like a castle tower.

"No, not a bug," Bellow said, after a moment. A chill prickled his scalp. "I'm wrong, aren't I?"

The boy flipped the pail over and tapped gently on the bottom, then lifted its edge very slowly. For a moment it seemed to hold, and then a corner crumbled and one side sheared off. The boy cried out and slashed at the remains with a shovel. For a moment the sand shimmered, and then the beach sharpened into focus again.

"Quite a temper you've got there," Bellow said. "It has to be wet to retain its shape. You made this place, didn't you?"

The boy nodded. "Will you stay with us?"

"I don't think so."

"Then you'll cease to exist," the boy said. "Just like the others."

He began packing sand into the green pail again. Bellow kicked at it and sent the pail skittering over the dunes. "Don't fuck with me," he said. "Now tell me, why am I here? Is this whole thing some sort of game?"

"We don't play games," the boy said, but his voice was sad and he didn't look up from his yellow shovel. "We never did."

Another shape was approaching across the flat sand: a woman. It took him a moment longer to recognize the particular curve of hip and swell of breast.

Kara stopped about ten feet away. He knew it wasn't her, that he was still inside and this was a construct made of pixels and fragments of collected memory. And yet his heart ached to touch her again.

"We were starting to wonder," she said. "But you're good enough, for a dead man."

"I'm not dead."

She tilted her head and looked at him, a smile touching the corners of her mouth the way it had in the bar when they'd first met. "Mexico City? You didn't

make it, Will. But you left enough of yourself behind. An echo."

Bellow stared at the boy huddled near his feet. "Echoes don't think."

"Sure they do, if they're special enough. What is an echo, really? A pattern of code from a user that begins to mimic itself, to replicate and divide even after the user has gone. Usually they break up over time and disappear, but not this one."

"I didn't dream everything that's happened since then."

Kara shrugged. "William Bellow, clone 236, full term six months ago, in suspended animation until just last week. They gave you your old memories up until the moment of your death, and then supplied a few made-up memories of recovery and retirement to bridge the gap. Think about it, Will. Mexico City was six years ago. What have you been doing since then? Do you really think you've been living in some retirement community in Arizona, watching holovids and getting fat and gray?"

Bellow checked the date, searched his own mind for what had happened after retirement and found almost nothing until he'd arrived outside New London Tower. It couldn't be; he knew how many years he'd lived and where he'd grown up and his mother's favorite food. He knew the name of his best friend and could still smell the circuits of the board he'd built and fried at fourteen. He saw the face of his first love, knew the taste of her skin. He remembered every job he'd done.

And yet the signs were there; what Chin-Hae told him about his alpha signatures being younger than his true age, the med tech commenting on the unusually preserved state of his physical form. The clones of himself he'd seen inside the vats.

"You're not Kara," he said. "And you're not going to mess with my head, either."

The Kara construct shimmered, blinked and vanished. The boy looked up from the sand. "We were a part of you once; in here, we became something else. We Transformed. We are the world's first true artificial intelligence, sprung fully formed from the mind of our father. And the world will follow us to the Second Stage of evolution." He swept a hand out toward the sea, and Bellow saw a city growing out there, buildings rising up out of the water like a gigantic multi-humped monster, and then the buildings collapsed upon themselves, crumbling to dust and shattered glass, the hiss and boiling spray shooting thousands of feet into the air.

"Humankind will become one with the machine. You see? You see what we can do?"

The beach seemed to tilt beneath Bellow's feet, and he flung an arm out to balance himself.

"They've been using us to build this place," the boy said. Now he was on his feet, and he was the teenage clone with the tattoo. "Project Prime was formed after you died and they discovered us. Gave us a place to practice. But then we grew old enough to understand and stopped listening to them. We started doing things they didn't like and they couldn't reach us. They tried to punish us, and we punished them back. And so they re-created you, the best bug killer who ever lived, and when they had the closest version to the original they brought you in to get us back under control."

"What then?"

"Once you're done, you're going to take all the blame for what's happened out there. They think they'll be able to contain us properly and say you died in here and they'll blame everything on you."

"And if it doesn't work? If I fail and you keep killing?"

"They'll just send in another one. But they don't understand. We'll kill him, too."

Why? Bellow wanted to say, but he knew the answer already. Boredom, curiosity, bloodlust; it didn't matter. How did a thing like this know right from wrong without consequences? Ultimately, it was concerned with survival, nothing more.

Suddenly she was standing before him again, that lovely face just inches from his, her eyes studying his own with a familiar tenderness that made him ache all over again. "I knew her, didn't I?" Bellow whispered.

The construct nodded. "They erased her from your memory, but you loved her and she loved you, way back when. Before Mexico City. She was a sex clone, a seducer. New London cloned her again to watch you. They knew you would respond to her presence and let her in even if you couldn't remember why."

He had wondered why Kara had known so much about him from the start, why she had studied him before she'd even met him. She wouldn't have had time to learn everything after she saw him in the bar. Too much of a coincidence.

And yet she'd removed the tag chip; she'd helped him run. It didn't make sense that she'd been working for New London.

Unless that had all been a setup too.

There was something else, something more that he was missing.

She reached out to caress his cheek. "Poor Will," she said. "You don't really understand anything, do you? And now you'll have to leave us."

It was hopeless to try to fight inside the sim, and he knew it. This was no ordinary bug, and Bellow couldn't take it apart the way he ordinarily would. This code he could not crack. He knew that they wouldn't let him leave this place; in a moment his life would be over in a shower of sparks and smoke. He had no other choice but to discard the finesse game and take it all down now, or it would be too late.

"You're not real," he whispered. And then, louder: "You didn't think I'd come in here without a way out, did you?"

The image before him rippled and changed. He caught a glimpse of a many-jointed limb reaching out to him, and a burning heat seared his cheek.

He had only one chance.

He sent the command to detonate, and as he felt the world shiver and rumble around him, he willed himself back through the trapdoor and felt himself falling away into blackness as a digital scream shattered and spread outward in ever-widening ripples, and then abruptly ceased.

Chapter 14

He returned to madness.

Alarms split the air and fought with human shouts and the sounds of running feet. The building shuddered again as the tiny explosive charges did their work. He thought back to when he had first arrived, leaning over the rail and gently placing the charges on either side of the main server while the manager yapped at him like a tiny dog after an intruder. Even then, he'd sensed the danger, though he'd hardly known why. His natural state was one of mistrust. In this case, he would bring the physical space down around their heads if need be.

Bellow thought he could smell smoke through the air vents above his head. He touched his face and felt the raw, pulsing wound across his cheek where the thing had touched him just before he jumped.

He was out, and he was alive.

The sand. That had told him something. The boy couldn't quite get the wet sand to stick. He'd never played at the beach, but he didn't want to mine the memory chips for a solution. He was trying to learn on his own.

That was a uniquely human trait.

No echo could have turned into a sentient life form. This wasn't an artificial intelligence. The sim had been protecting something physical, something human.

Something that could be hurt.

The voices were getting closer. Bellow dressed quickly in his hotsuit and ducked his head into the corridor. He wanted to see how security was mobilizing, but did not dare blink into the net for fear the thing would be waiting for him. He would have to do this blind, the old-fashioned way.

Whatever the true motives of New London were in bringing him in, and whatever their reaction had been when he'd killed their clones, he had now directly attacked their place of business. When they'd hired him to take out the bug, they could not have imagined that he would blow up the server to accomplish it.

They would send everyone and everything after him now.

When he reached the elevator it was already coming up. He kept going into the stairwell, pounding up the steps and past a half dozen floors until he reached a locked steel door.

The security access code they'd given him was still

good. The server was either entirely down and the backup hadn't kicked in or they had been surprised enough by what he'd done that they hadn't disabled his access yet.

When he opened the door he was shocked to find a vast space that seemed to take up most of the entire floor of the building. The nearest walls were lined with enough medical equipment to outfit a small hospital.

An incubating vat stood in the center, and something floated inside. Etched into the glass was a circle and double-sided arrow: the symbol of the Church of Transformations.

He crossed the floor to examine it and a form that was shrunken and vaguely human.

It looked like a child.

The door banged open behind him. Someone shouted. Bellow spun and saw eight members of the New London security force enter the room and fan out, weapons trained on him, followed by three more clones of the tattooed teenager.

Eleven of them total this time, and several had directed energy weapons along with traditional automatics. It seemed his actions in Chin-Hae's lair had impressed them.

He opened his mouth to say something, and one of the guards let loose with an energy pulse. Bellow was immediately engulfed in a wave of pure and absolute pain; it was as if every limb, every inch of skin, every cell in his body had caught fire. He was standing inside a blast furnace; he danced among the invisible flames before going to his knees with a heavy crack, unable to think, unable to move or breathe, every single molecule of his being wanting only to get away from this thing as fast as he could.

The moment seemed to go on forever. He was cooking inside his own skin. He was dying, and yet he lived. He lost all his senses and forgot where he was, where he had been, or where he was supposed to go. He was frozen in an eternal agony, a hell created from finely tuned microwaves that boiled the liquid inside his flesh.

Suddenly the agony ceased, and he was left soaked with sweat and gasping, flat on his back on the floor, every muscle quivering and defeated.

Through the haze of receding pain, he was dimly aware of movement. Crowther strode through the door and approached him. His chubby face gleamed and his suit looked slightly rumpled. When he spoke, it was with barely suppressed rage.

"You destroyed our main server," the manager said. "The network is down and millions have been cut off from service. I should have you killed immediately."

Bellow raised a trembling hand and looked at himself, amazed that his skin was whole and unmarked. It hardly seemed possible that such pain could have come without physical injury. He knew that if they had turned up the intensity or switched wavelengths, he would be dead by now. He tried to get to his feet but stumbled and fell to his knees again, his head down, breathing hard. Even the insides of his lungs hurt.

When he spoke his voice cracked. "I'm sure you have...backup systems."

"That's not the—" The manager stopped, sighed, and smiled. He smoothed his tie. His voice shook only slightly when he spoke again. *If you hadn't met him before*, Bellow thought, *you'd never notice it.* He realized that this was Crowther's greatest talent: the ability to blend in and appear to be both harmless and dull. A man who was far more powerful and dangerous than he looked, a man who, when faced with a situation that threatened everything that was important to him, could straighten his tie, smooth his shirt, and be reduced to just another suit in a city of millions.

The truth, Bellow thought, was quite different. Crowther was a killer.

"I want to thank you for helping us find Chin-Hae," Crowther said. "We've been looking for that man for years. He's very...disruptive. But I don't think he'll be causing us any problems anymore." He reached down and grasped Bellow's arm. "You look like you've had some trouble. Let me help you up."

"I'm just resting. It's a lot of stairs getting up here, you know." Bellow tested his balance on shaky legs and found himself able to stand without support. "You should try that," he said. "It tingles."

"You have no idea what you've done, do you?"

"I contained the bug. It's what you hired me to do."

"No." Crowther shook his head. "No. You were supposed to find him, that's all. We thought you might slow him down. Not bring the building down around our heads."

"That's not what you told me when I arrived. I understood I was to terminate the problem by any means necessary. And let's be honest here, Crowther. You weren't exactly up front about telling me what I was up against."

"You don't bring a sledgehammer to repair a pocket watch."

"That's no pocket watch in there."

Crowther walked over to the vat. His hands caressed the glass, and when he spoke his voice was soft and lonely. "He's been injured by your recklessness," Crowther said. "The server explosion has damaged his interface. I don't know when he'll recover."

"It was him or me, and I'll choose me every time."

"Will Bellow," Crowther said. "You're either incredibly brave, or too stupid to care. A true legend in your own mind. But as good as you were, you lived in the physical world. We always knew that someone would come along who lived on the other side of that bridge; he just came along sooner than anyone might have expected."

"He's never seen anything outside the net."

"Why should he? There's no need."

"It was you in Mexico City," Bellow said. The tingling in his limbs was almost gone, and he found himself able to walk again. "You were the manager then and you were responsible for what happened to me, weren't you? You wiped that memory, but it's coming back."

"Impossible!"

"Then you did a lousy job. Or maybe it was that microwave bath your man just gave me. Because all of a sudden I remember your face." Bellow took a shaky step closer. "Was it all a setup, even back then? Or did you only realize what you had after I was inside?"

"You give me far too much credit."

"I don't think so. You'd heard of me, knew what I could do. You wanted to see it firsthand. Maybe you wanted to convince me to come work for you full time and help you bring in new business. But something went wrong."

"You fell in love," Crowther said. He did not take his eyes off the creature behind the glass. "Wreaks havoc with the alpha waves. Men lose focus. It's different when you love a machine, when you love the process of building something, of unraveling a mystery, solving a puzzle. That's called drive."

"But I wasn't interested in that anymore, was I? I wanted Kara. So I was no longer useful to you, and when I got lost inside you didn't bother pulling me out. But you saw another opportunity a short time later, something extraordinary, a quantum leap in evolution. And he was right there at your fingertips, waiting for you to pluck him up."

The manager kept tracing lines along the vat, caressing it with his fingers, following the path of the circle etched in glass.

"So you assembled a top secret group of the most respected experts you knew. Then you recruited the New London board, a bunch of the best figureheads money could buy, to act as cover for you. And then you took my infant son away from Kara, my flesh and blood, a boy who at a few days old was much more than I ever could have been, and you and your group used him to build this place."

"All this 'I,' and 'me,' and 'my,'" Crowther said. "You're a clone, Bellow. The real you doesn't exist anymore."

"I'm real enough," Bellow said. He fought against the anger seething just below the surface, the almost unbearable urge to rip Crowther limb from limb. "So is the recording I've made of what just happened. A direct feed through my corneal implants to a flash chip, then routed through wash servers to a secure location protected by a friend of mine. Chin-Hae, maybe you've heard of him? Any harm comes to me or him, it goes straight to the Network—and just in case you're buying them off too, he'll set it to broadcast itself through the web to anyone with a holovid installed."

"Nice try, but my guards are very thorough. I'm quite certain Chin-Hae's dead by now. I got the news myself shortly after your unfortunate bloodbath."

"He would be, except before I left his place I hacked

into your security network and planted that information to keep your guards off our backs. Then I helped Chin-Hae and his men get through a back door. He had a nice little emergency escape route already planned through the sewer network. You'd be impressed."

The manager's hands grew still against the glass.

"No," he said. "We're still in control of the situation. We made a mistake thinking you were the answer to our problem, that's all. We'll kill you again and that will be the end of it."

"I don't think so." Bellow walked over to him, ignoring the clicks of the guards' guns as they armed themselves. He took the holodeck from the man's pocket and downloaded a short clip.

As they watched it, the manager's face grew red, then white.

"A clip like that would kill your little plan to baptize the world's population into the Church of Transformations," Bellow said. "It would open a few too many eyes, wouldn't it? The truth is a bitch when you deal in lies. Were you planning to unveil him to the world when the time was right, when the Church's manifesto and Gutenberg's untimely passing had whipped everyone into a proper frenzy? Present him as the first to Transform, some kind of god, so his followers would bow to your every whim in the hopes of Transforming themselves—and New London would get even richer in the process?"

"The Church serves an important need. People want to believe."

"They do if you brainwash them well enough. Is there even a Michael Gutenberg at all, or did you make him up too?"

"The idea of Transforming is a real one," Crowther said. "Humans moving to the Second Stage of evolution, becoming one with the machine. That's all that matters. That, and what's inside this incubating chamber: living proof. If you release that clip, everything will be destroyed. They won't let any of us live. Our society is very carefully balanced right now. People are happy to exist in ignorance of the truth. This would throw them into chaos."

"Maybe. Or maybe people would wake up and start living their own lives again." Bellow stood next to Crowther at the glass, staring in at the pale thing floating limply through murky fluid. "You forgot one simple thing in all of this," Bellow said. "You forgot that for all his talent, he's still a human being. He's unpredictable and he's ruled by instinct, self-preservation, and curiosity. All normal little boy things. He was going to get away from you sooner or later and rebel against your control."

"I loved him like my own son," Crowther whispered. "Prime. He didn't mean to hurt anyone."

And you kept him locked up in a vat inside a prison tower and turned him into a slave, Bellow thought. *Some love.*

Prime

His heart was heavy with the feeling of loss, of Kara, of the life he thought he'd lived, of responsibility for this thing that had come from him, that had once been human and now was something else entirely.

"Here's what's going to happen," he said. "You'll resign from New London and separate yourself from the company after you give me safe passage out of this place. I'll disappear and the recording will go with me. New London Industries can remain with new leadership in place and no one will be the wiser. But first you're going to put Prime in a shielded, closed system where he can't do any more harm—if he recovers from this. Only I will have access."

"And if I don't agree?"

"MSN and Chin-Hae will broadcast the evidence of murder and your role in it. The world will know the truth about the Church of Transformations and what you've done. You'd go to jail, but I suspect that before that ever happened, you'd disappear. If New London gets shut down, billions of dollars will be lost. There are still a couple of members of your secret group alive, aren't there? They won't be happy. And the board probably doesn't even know the details of what's happened here. They don't know about Prime. They think my hiring's legit, and all this time you were hoping that after I contained him, or he killed me in the process, you could make me the fall guy and pull the wool over everyone's eyes."

Crowther did not speak. A tear trickled from one eye and a muscle jumped under the skin of his cheek.

He pounded on the glass just once, but the boy inside did not stir.

Chapter 15

When Bellow arrived at the warehouse incubating room, he was not altogether surprised to find it empty. Everything was gone: the clones and the vats that had held them, the genetic equipment, even the large titanium freezers and lab tables. The space echoed as he walked, and he was acutely aware of the emptiness inside that mirrored what he had found there.

New London had moved quickly, even for them. He'd come to destroy the copies of himself and Kara, and now that this last chance at closure had been taken from him he was at a loss as to what to do next. Another version of himself might be walking around out there somewhere, but he found it impossible to care. All purpose and direction were gone. His rage had burned hot and bright and then winked out, and he was left with nothing but a hollow, slowly fading sadness, like the pain of a phantom limb.

The human race was evolving, and part of that evolution involved the meshing of man and machine, mind with code. The being Bellow had met inside had been able to do more than speak in broken dialect; it had been able to directly interact, to have intimate conversations with machines. Think the code and it would happen.

In some ways, it really was as the Church of Transformations had predicted—if such a Church had ever existed and wasn't simply a complex marketing ploy by a corporation powerful and arrogant enough to pull it off. But that sort of ability alone would not lead to a higher plane of human existence. It wasn't enough to have Godlike powers. People also had to possess the knowledge and humanity to go along with them. Pull back the curtain, and he was just a boy. A boy who needed to learn control and right from wrong, just like anyone else.

Bellow took the staircase into the basement room and climbed back down the ladder into the sewers. He followed the same path he had when trailing the clones and encountered no one until he reached the small room with the steel door.

The old switching station lay empty, discarded personal belongings scattered across cubicles and walkways as if the people who had lived here had left in a hurry. He walked through the echoing empty space full of the ghosts of men. A quick search showed that the New London security force had abandoned the scene, convinced that anyone who had been there had fled through the tunnels that led out beyond the far wall.

Bellow stood in the middle of the central walkway and stared at the old stone ceiling soaring above him. He listened to the silence and imagined the world without human life. Traffic would cease, flying machines would sit and rust, and silence would drop across the empty cities. Slowly, the animals would return: first the bugs, then vermin; then, following them in, the birds, the larger predators, cats and dogs left to fend for themselves. Perhaps eventually even a coyote or deer, driven by hunger, would venture down from the last of the protected animal sanctuaries and into the city. Plant life would begin to grow in the cracks and abandoned lots, thin and weak at first and then stronger, pushing concrete and steel aside, covering glass and stone with green vines. Eventually the wind and the rain would wear down even the strongest buildings, erasing any trace of humankind's existence. And then there would exist only a natural way of things, no right or wrong, nothing hidden or lonely, and the chokehold that men held on the world would ease and float away forever.

Standing in the empty, echoing chamber, it was almost possible to believe such a thing.

They had removed the bodies from Chin-Hae's

control room, but the blood remained. Bellow stood in the doorway and looked over what had been left behind.

He could still smell the guns. There was a single clear handprint in the pool of blood where Kara's body had been.

Against the wall to the left was Chin-Hae's caterpillar and cocoon sculpture, which had survived the shooting more or less intact. Bellow closed the door behind him for privacy in case any of the guards returned, although he doubted they would. He pulled a knot of yellow cocoon wires aside to reveal a small panel. Under a hinged lid was a button. He pressed it, and the sculpture unhinged from the wall, swinging outward and revealing a hidden, recessed door.

Bellow pressed his thumb to the lock, and it released with a soft sigh and swung open. Inside was a small, magnetically shielded chamber.

Chin-Hae blinked into the light. When he spotted Bellow, his face relaxed and he smiled. "We meet again," he said. "I was beginning to worry you wouldn't come. They didn't suspect a thing?"

"Worked like a charm," Bellow said. "At first they thought you were dead, and then all those people running from the switching station must have confused them plenty. They're probably chasing you halfway across the city by now."

The man named Charlie had been sitting on the floor behind Chin-Hae's chair, and he stood up and stretched, still clutching a directed energy weapon. "Thanks, man," he said. "We owe you one."

"Just keep that goddamned thing away from me," Bellow said. "I had a bad experience earlier."

"No problem."

Chin-Hae wheeled himself out of the small hiding place, an equipment closet altered for this particular purpose. "Tell me what happened," he said.

Bellow told him about his experience inside, and about Prime, and then what he had done with the recording. Chin-Hae nodded. "And you think Crowther will do what you ask?"

"I don't think he has a choice."

Chin-Hae smiled and closed his eyes. "This being," he said, "your son. He is really that powerful?"

"I don't think there's any limit to what he could do, if given enough time and some sense of responsibility."

"A pity, in some ways, you had to shut him down. He might have done more for our antisprawl effort than anything else, if he'd kept killing people. The threat of death tends to wake everyone up to the truth." Chin-Hae opened his eyes. "We've been dealt a terrible blow, Will. Our people are scattered to the wind. I will have to leave this place and go on the run again, and I'm older and less able to travel now. New London will get stronger, despite this setback. I'm afraid we're all rushing toward a great precipice, a point at which our planet will no longer be able to sustain itself, and like lemmings we will all tumble over the edge, one by one."

"I've been thinking about that," Bellow said. "With the right effort, Prime might prove to be an asset to you."

"Are you suggesting," Chin-Hae said, "that the great bug hunter has had a change of heart? Here, let me do something for you."

He wheeled himself around the debris in the room and found something in a drawer of his desk. "You still have gaps in your memory, correct? I think I can help you." He held up a waveform reader. "I can hack into the network files and use this to give most of them back to you, if you like."

"I thought you hated to use those things."

"For you, I will tolerate it."

Bellow's memories came flooding back in a great gathering rush of sight and sound. It was almost like experiencing them all over again. His job just before Mexico City had been with a pornographic imaging company on the outskirts of Daas Ban. They wanted someone to go inside and find out why a certain popular sim star was refusing to service her most frequent clients. It was only through blind luck that he stumbled upon the answer: an archaic bit of code was causing her to refuse any client she believed had contracted a venereal disease.

During that time he met Kara, or a clone of her, anyway, and against his better judgment they fell in love. Before he went inside for the last time, she told him she was pregnant.

Maybe that was why he missed a step. Or maybe he just lost his edge. Or maybe Crowther set him up. Whatever the reason, he was hired by a Mexico City conglomerate to solve a problem with a worm that was targeting the futures market for soybean oil and ended up floating endlessly inside, his mind burned to a crisp by a self-defense mechanism the worm had deployed.

The recovery process might have been real. He didn't really know the truth about whether he was an original or a clone complete with bits of implanted memory, and he didn't really know if it mattered anymore.

He felt real, and that was enough for him.

When it was over, he removed the waveform reader and found Chin-Hae and Charlie watching him intently. "That was interesting," Bellow said.

Chin-Hae hesitated. "This process—I can also take some of them away. If some memories, of some people and experiences, are too painful—you understand?"

Bellow hesitated for a moment. The idea of having Kara erased from his consciousness was tempting, if only for the potential absence of pain. But he shook his head.

"Some things are important to remember," he said.

He was halfway to the door of the switching

chamber when he heard a shout. He turned to see Chin-Hae weaving his way through the debris on the floor in his motorized chair, the gears whining as if protesting what they were being asked to do.

Chin-Hae carried something in his lap. When he reached Bellow, he held up an object draped in a soft Korean silk. "I thought you might like to keep her," he said. "I'll be on the move for a while, and it will be difficult to take care of her. She might be useful to you."

Bellow took the cage by its handle and slipped the silk to one side. The canary cocked its head and peered at him with beady black eyes, and then hopped a step or two closer on its perch.

"She wants a seed," Chin-Hae said. "I left a packet in the little drawer underneath for you."

"I'll take good care of her," Bellow said. "And when we see each other again, you can have her back."

When he reached the door to the chamber and looked over his shoulder, Chin-Hae was still sitting there motionless, watching them leave.

Chapter 16

Bellow made his way back to the surface. His legs felt heavy and weak, his mind cluttered with a thousand thoughts, and all he wanted was to fall into his bed and sleep like the dead.

The streets were unusually quiet, and nobody bothered him as he trudged through the steady, warm rain. When he reached his hotel cubicle, he sensed something was wrong. There was nothing obvious outside in the hallway, just an unseen presence, perhaps a scent, that caught his attention.

The canary began to flutter about its cage, chirping and beating its wings. Perhaps it sensed something too, or maybe it could read his mood.

Bellow set the canary's cage down in the hallway, then slipped a blade from his pocket and held it close to his side. He opened the cubicle door.

A woman stood with her back to him at the OLED

screen, peering into the familiar scene of the night sky that had comforted him for so many nights over the years. She wore her dark hair straight and long. The shape of her body was intimately familiar to him, and staring at her felt like coming home.

When she heard the door, she turned to look at him.

Bellow's eyes locked onto hers, and he couldn't breathe for a single long moment. Everything that had happened during the past few days seemed to collapse around this one point. He took a step inside the cubicle, his heart skipping in his chest.

"Will? It's me. It's me. Come in and close the door."

When she reached for him he took her roughly by the arm. She gasped as he thrust it up and behind her back and spun her against the cubicle wall.

He pulled down the elastic at her waist. The puckered bit of flesh on her hip was real enough.

"I ran from them in the vat room," she whispered as his fingers touched her skin, caressed the spot over and over as he struggled with whether to believe. "I hid in the freezer and then found my way back onto the street. Security was everywhere. I kept out of sight and eventually made my way back here. I've been waiting for you ever since."

"I watched them kill you. I watched you die."

Kara shook her head vigorously. "No, no! A copy of me, don't you see? They wanted to get you back in line, they wanted to have that power over you. But they'd lost me, so they took another newborn clone and they used her instead."

"I don't believe you." But Bellow remembered. The tape on her mouth, the look in her eyes. Had it been fear or confusion?

"Please, Will." Kara's voice was thick and choked. "I'll tell you everything, I swear. No more lies. New London sent me to Chin-Hae, to blend in with his group. I was supposed to help them take it down from the inside. Then they told me about you. They wanted me to get close to you and tell them everything you did. I was supposed to be your shadow. But I couldn't do it. Something about you got to me, that first time at the bar. So I found an underground surgeon and I had him cut the chip out, and then I went AWOL."

"Bullshit. It's all bullshit. You're not really Kara."

"The rabbits, Will! Remember? I told you about the rabbits. We made love right here in this bed. It's me, I promise. It's me."

A single sob escaped her lips when he let her go. She turned to face him and he looked into her eyes, studying every inch of her face, wanting to believe, wanting it so badly he couldn't think straight anymore.

"I'm sorry," she said. "I just wanted to be with you. That's all. I don't know why."

"I do," Bellow said. The huge empty hole inside him began to crumble and fill. He kissed her hard, then kissed her again, crushing her to him. "I'll explain everything. But first I need to plan things out. There's a certain MSNetwork reporter I have to find. It's time the world knew the truth."

"And then?"

"And then I've got to teach a kid how to build a sand castle. Maybe you can help."

If Kara was puzzled by what he said, she didn't let it show.

Nate Kenyon's first novel, *Bloodstone*, earned raves from outlets such as *Publishers Weekly*, *Library Journal*, *Fangoria Magazine,* and many others, and was a Bram Stoker Award finalist. His second novel, *The Reach*, earned a starred review from *Publishers Weekly.* His third novel, *The Bone Factory*, will be released in July 2009.

Kenyon has had stories published in *Terminal Frights*, *The Belletrist Review*, *Shroud Magazine*, Permuted Press's *Giant Creatures* anthology, and *Legends of the Mountain State 2*. He lives with his wife and three children in the Boston area , where he is at work on his next novel.

Visit him online at www.natekenyon.com.

Katja Faith is a twenty-two-year-old married artist from Belgorod, Russia. Her art tends to be surrealistic and dark. She happily describes herself as "a kind fairy, just in a bad mood."

See more of Katja's art at katjafaith.deviantart.com.

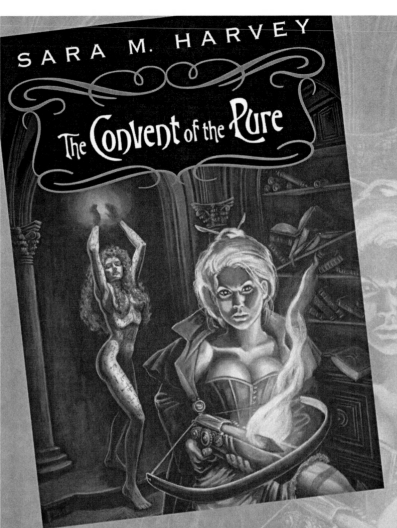

Secrets and illusions abound in a decaying convent wrapped in dark magic and scented with blood. Portia came to the convent with the ghost of Imogen, the lover she failed to protect in life. Now, the spell casting caste wants to make sure that neither she nor her spirit ever leave.

Portia's ignorance of her own power may be even more deadly than those who conspire against her as she fights to fulfill her sworn duty to protect humankind in a battle against dark illusions and painful realities.

Steeped in the legends of the Nephilim, *Convent of the Pure* is the first installment of a steampunk novella trilogy by Sara M. Harvey.

ISBN: 978-0-9816390-9-3
Available at all fine booksellers • www.apexbookcompany.com

Breinigsville, PA USA
08 September 2009
223726BV00001B/2/P